KWAME

P9-AQA-255

"May I see some identification?" said the uniformed security guard.

"Not until we know what's going on!" said Kwame. He surprised himself with his flare of temper. But he felt bullied by this guard.

"I'd like the two of you to turn out your pockets, and you, miss, please place the contents of your purse here," said the guard, holding out a wooden tray.

Marcia opened her purse and dumped the contents of it on the tray.

18 Pine St.

Kwame's Girl

Written by
Stacie Johnson

Created by
WALTER DEAN MYERS

A Seth Godin Production

BANTAM BOOKS
NEW YORK · TORONTO · LONDON · SYDNEY · AUCKLAND

RL 5, age 10 and up

KWAME'S GIRL
A Bantam Book / March 1994

Thanks to Susan Korman, Betsy Gould, Amy Berkower, Fran Lebowitz, Marva Martin, Michael Cader, Megan O'Connor, José Arroyo, Julie Maner, Chris Angelilli, Ellen Kenny, Helene and Lucy Wood.

18 Pine St. is a trademark of Seth Godin Productions, Inc.

ISBN 0-553-56313-0

Published simultaneously in the United States and Canada

Bantam Books are published by Bantam Books, a division of Bantam Doubleday Dell Publishing Group, Inc. Its trademark, consisting of the words "Bantam Books" and the portrayal of a rooster, is Registered in U.S. Patent and Trademark Office and in other countries. Marca Registrada. Bantam Books, 1540 Broadway, New York, New York 10036.

PRINTED IN THE UNITED STATES OF AMERICA

OPM 0 9 8 7 6 5 4 3 2 1

For Michael

18 Pine St.

There is a card shop at 8 Pine St., and a shop that sells sewing supplies at 10 Pine that's only open in the afternoons and on Saturdays if it doesn't rain. For some reason that no one seems to know or care about, there is no 12, 14, or 16 Pine. The name of the pizzeria at 18 Pine St. was Antonio's before Mr. and Mrs. Harris took it over. Mr. Harris removed Antonio's sign and just put up a sign announcing the address. By the time he got around to thinking of a name for the place, everybody was calling it 18 Pine.

The Crew at 18 Pine St.

Sarah Gordon is the heart and soul of the group. Sarah's pretty, with a great smile and a warm, caring attitude that makes her a terrific friend. Sarah's the reason that everyone shows up at 18 Pine St.

Tasha Gordon, tall, sexy, and smart, is Sarah's cousin. Since her parents died four years ago, Tasha has moved from relative to relative. Now she's living with Sarah and her family—maybe for good.

Cindy Phillips is Sarah's best friend. Cindy is petite, with dark, radiant skin and a cute nose. She wears her black hair in braids. Cindy's been Sarah's neighbor and friend since she moved from Jamaica when she was three.

Kwame Brown's only a sophomore, but that doesn't stop him from being part of the crew. As the smartest kid in the group, he's the one Jennifer turns to for help with her homework.

Jennifer Wilson is the poor little rich girl. Her parents are divorced, and all the charge cards and clothes in the world can't make up for it. Jennifer's tall and thin, with cocoa-colored skin and a body that's made for all those designer clothes she wears.

April Winter has been to ten schools in the last ten years—and she hopes she's at Murphy to stay. Her energy, blond hair, and offbeat personality make her a standout at school.

And there's Dave Hunter, Brian Wu, and the rest of the gang. You'll meet them all in the halls of Murphy High and after school for a pizza at 18 Pine St.

One

"I'm sick of it already!" April Winter groaned. She blew a strand of blond hair away from her eyes and stared glumly at the snow that spun in the wind outside the 18 Pine St. pizzeria.

"I love it," said Cindy Phillips, pointing to the windows before she dipped a tortilla chip in the salsa. "My cousins in Jamaica would freak if they saw snow."

"Oh, I like the snow," said April, turning to her friend. "I was talking about the new school term."

Kwame Brown lowered his head and looked at April over the tops of his dark-rimmed glasses. "How can you be sick of school already? We've only been back at Murphy High for a week! I was bored out of my skull the last few days of vacation. I saw everything on TV—twice!"

Cindy nodded. "I read all my mom's mystery novels."

"Okay, maybe it got a little dull toward the end," April admitted, "but I'll bet you both miss sleeping late." She lowered her voice to a soft whisper. "Remember when you woke up early? Then you realized you were on vacation, and you turned the pillow over, pulled the covers up to your chin, and drifted slooooowly back to sleep...."

Cindy covered her mouth and yawned loudly.

"Okay, okay," Kwame protested.

April picked up a tortilla chip and settled back. "I rest my case."

When Sarah Gordon and her cousin Tasha arrived, Kwame slid over in the booth to make room for them.

"Thanks, Kwame." Tasha flashed him a grateful smile and sat down next to him.

As Tasha removed her coat, Kwame caught a whiff of her perfume, mixed with the fresh cold air she had brought in. Kwame had been interested in Tasha ever since she'd moved to Madison earlier in the year. Her parents had been killed in a car accident several years ago, and now she lived with Sarah's family. With her smooth brown skin and curly hair that rippled past her shoulder blades, Tasha dazzled everyone who looked at her, especially Billy Simpson, the captain of Murphy High's football team. Kwame knew he could never compete with Billy, but he could still admire Tasha from afar. He especially liked her eyes, which could flash with temper one minute and glitter with

2

good humor the next.

Sarah Gordon was more even-tempered than her pretty cousin. There was something about her warm smile and large brown eyes that put people at ease. Kwame remembered how Sarah had taken April under her wing when the sophomore first moved to Madison. In her old school, April had not known many black people. Now Sarah and Tasha were two of her closest friends.

Tasha winked at Cindy and April, then turned to Kwame with an innocent expression. "Hey, Kwame, have you met Marcia Dean yet?"

"Marcia who?" asked Kwame.

"Marcia Dean," Sarah repeated. "She's a new girl. She just moved to Madison a couple weeks ago. She hasn't been at our lunch table because she's been meeting with her guidance counselor all this week to get her schedule straightened out and adjust to the new school."

"I asked her to stop by 18 Pine today since she doesn't know anybody yet," said Tasha.

"You talking about Marcia Dean?" said Jennifer Wilson, coming up to their booth. Jennifer took off her long leather coat slowly, giving her friends plenty of time to admire it.

"Gorgeous coat," said Sarah, touching the heavy black sleeve.

"My dad got it for me in England," said Jennifer as she pulled a chair toward the booth. Mr. and Mrs. Wilson were divorced, and Jennifer always got expensive

3

gifts from her father around the holidays. Even if no holidays were coming up, Jennifer could always buy what she liked by using one of the many credit cards she owned.

"I saw Marcia after class," Jennifer announced. "She said she'd stop by." When Jennifer saw what Kwame was eating, she gasped and put her hand on his forehead. "Kwame, are you all right?"

"Of course," said Kwame. "Do I look sick to you?"

Jennifer laughed. "No, but you're not eating pizza, so I figured something must be wrong."

"No more pizza for a while," said Kwame. "I'm saving my money for a bayonet."

Kwame's friends were not surprised by his reply. Even though he got A's in every class, Kwame's favorite subject was history. He knew more dates and battles than anyone else at Murphy High, including the teachers, some students suspected.

"Is this another one of your Civil War souvenirs?" asked Cindy. "Your room must look like a barracks!"

"Revolutionary War, actually," Kwame corrected her. He leaned across the table and looked excitedly at his friends. "There's a place in Kentucky that makes replicas of the original arms used in the Revolutionary War. I wanted a musket, but it was too expensive."

"And the cannon was too heavy to mail!" said Cindy. She and the others broke into laughter.

"But you didn't save any money by buying the nachos," Tasha pointed out. "They cost more than one slice of pizza."

4

"Yeah," Kwame replied with a grin, "but when have you ever seen me eat just *one* slice of pizza?"

"Oops, I forgot who I was talking to!" said Tasha. Kwame's appetite for pizza was legendary. When the gang put their money together and bought a large pie, Kwame would finish his first slice while his friends were waiting for theirs to cool.

With six hands going into the basket of tortilla chips, it was empty in no time. Sarah took it back to the counter and waited for Mr. Harris, the owner of the pizzeria, to refill it.

"April is sick of school," Cindy told Tasha.

"Already?" said Tasha.

"You would be, too, if you had five assignments due on Monday," said April. "The only class I don't have homework in is gym class! Who do those teachers think we are?"

"Students!" Kwame replied. "Would you rather be doing homework, or working a job?"

"At least you get paid to do a job," said April.

"Now that you mention it, April, it has been a pretty tough week. I have two quizzes on Monday to study for," said Cindy, making a face.

"Does that mean you won't be going to the mall with us tomorrow?" Sarah asked, returning with the basket of chips.

Cindy snorted. "I said quizzes, not the SAT's! I'll be there!"

"What about you, cuz, are you still on for our assault on the Westcove Mall?" Sarah asked Tasha.

"You can count me in," her cousin replied. She craned her neck to look toward the front door. "We can ask Marcia to come, too. If she ever shows up."

"What's this new girl like?" said Kwame.

Tasha smiled at him and patted his shoulder. "She's very nice," she said. "I'll make sure to introduce you."

"We know she's new in town," added Cindy. "So she can't be going out with anybody yet." She raised her eyebrows meaningfully at Kwame.

"And she's a junior, so she's an older woman," said Jennifer, raising her eyebrows as well.

"Very funny!" said Kwame, flustered. "I just asked a simple question." He felt even more embarrassed when Sarah came to his defense.

"Don't let them bug you, Kwame," said Sarah. "I'd like to know more about her, too."

"She's from Philadelphia," said Tasha. "And she's in my English class, so she's got to be smart."

"The girl has style, too," said Jennifer. "She's in my math class, and she's worn a different pair of earrings with a matching bracelet every day this week."

"Sounds like a girl I want to meet," a familiar voice called out. The gang was surprised to see Billy Simpson standing next to their booth. Lately Billy had been busy after school, and no one was sure what he was up to. He smiled at everyone as he set the paper plate with his pizza slice on the table. Then he dragged a chair from a nearby table and sat down next to Tasha.

"Nice of you to join us," said Tasha sarcastically.

Billy bit off a slice of pizza. "I can only stay a

minute," he said in a hoarse voice.

"Then you're off to your mystery job, right?" said Tasha.

Billy nodded.

"And you're not going to tell us what it is, right?" continued Tasha.

Billy nodded again.

"Must be something illegal," said Jennifer.

Billy laughed, then shrugged his muscular shoulders. "Maybe," he said, with a mysterious smile.

"I can't believe you're keeping secrets from your friends." April shook her head.

"Yeah, you owe us an explanation," said Cindy.

"Listen," said Billy, putting his pizza down and frowning at Cindy and Tasha. He cleared his throat, but his voice still came out strained. "I don't know every little detail about your lives, so why should you know all about mine?"

"Because this isn't something personal," Tasha pointed out.

"How do you know?" Billy challenged. "It could be something I don't feel comfortable talking about. You-all have to respect my right to privacy."

"If you're just going to a part-time job, like you say you are, there's no reason to keep it a secret," said Cindy.

"Unless it's something illegal," Jennifer repeated.

Billy sighed loudly. "What do you think, Kwame?" He turned toward his friend. "Do you think I owe them an explanation?"

7

Kwame felt Tasha looking at him intently. "I'm curious," he admitted as Tasha smiled. "But it's also none of my business."

"Thanks a lot, Kwame," muttered Tasha, turning away.

Billy finished his pizza and left a few minutes later. As he made his way to the front of the pizzeria, he almost bumped into a thin black girl who stood by the door, looking around.

Jennifer spotted the thin girl and waved her to the back booth. "She's here," she announced.

Kwame turned to see the new girl his friends were eager for him to meet. Even from a distance, he could see that Marcia had unusual eyes. He had seen only a handful of blacks with gray eyes, and never anyone as pretty as Marcia was. Her hair was short and combed away from her face, which made her cheekbones look strong, almost Indian. She wore light blue jeans with black leggings poking through the rips and holes. Under her oversize Chicago Bulls jacket, she had on a brightly colored sweater. Kwame looked away before she could catch him staring at her.

When Marcia came over, Jennifer introduced her to Kwame and April. Kwame motioned her to the chair where Billy had been sitting moments before.

"How do you like Madison so far?" asked April as the new girl sat down.

Marcia laughed nervously as she glanced through the picture windows at the front of the pizzeria. "It's very different from Philly, I'll tell you that," she said.

"You mean smaller and boring, right?" asked Tasha. "Believe me, that's how I felt when I moved here from Oakland. Give it a chance, though; this place will grow on you."

"Truth is, I haven't seen much of Madison yet," Marcia admitted. " We've been pretty busy getting settled in the new house."

"Do you like Murphy High so far?" asked Kwame.

"Yeah," said Marcia, fixing her dark gray eyes on him. "It's about half the size of the school I went to in Philly, but I still need to learn my way around."

"You'll do fine if you remember to stay out of Mr. Schlesinger's way," said Jennifer. The others nodded.

"He's the vice-principal," Sarah explained. "And he's got the loudest voice in the state! If he ever yells at you, you're going to know it!"

Marcia smiled. "Sounds like my dad," she said.

"There's two other things you ought to learn right away," said Cindy, counting on her fingers. "Mr. Cala, the math teacher, is the toughest grader in the school, and Mr. Sanchez's Spanish class is the easiest."

"Mr. Kelly will let you out of his gym class if you tell him you're having your period," said April, adding her own advice. "But Mrs. Zimmer won't, so don't even try it."

"I'll try to remember that," said Marcia, laughing.

"Have you started the English assignment?" Tasha asked her. "Ms. Bender wants us to write an essay," she explained to the others. "The title has to be 'New Year's Resolutions to Save the Earth.'"

"Mention recycling," said Kwame.

"Got it already," said Tasha. "Any other ideas?" She pulled a notebook from her book bag and took out a shiny gold pen.

"Nice pen," said Jennifer admiringly. "I saw those at Samuel's Stationery."

Tasha picked up the pen and pointed at Sarah. "My grandmother gave us each a pen-and-pencil set for Christmas. I can't get used to the mechanical pencil, but this," she said, waving the pen, "is my new baby."

"Pens!" said Cindy with a chuckle. "That's a 'Grandma' kind of gift. That and sweaters."

"That's how I got this," said Marcia, pointing at the yellow, blue, and orange sweater she wore.

"You're all lucky," said Kwame with a sigh. "My grandmother bought me a bow tie!" He pursed his lips and mimicked his grandmother. "'Don't wear it to school, child, this bow tie is for church on Sunday!'"

Kwame watched as Marcia covered her mouth and laughed with the others at his imitation. When she looked at him again, her eyes were shiny from laughing, and Kwame felt his stomach flutter.

Marcia suddenly looked at her watch. "Dang!" she said, reaching for her coat. "I have to get home. We still have a lot to unpack. I wish I hadn't gotten lost on the way over here."

"Do you need any help?" said Kwame, standing up. He felt stupid the minute he said it, but Marcia smiled at him.

"No, but thanks," she said. "All I need to know is

which bus will take me to Fairview Heights from here."

Kwame's face brightened. "That's on my bus line," he replied. "It's the Number Fourteen. You get it across the street."

"Thanks...um..."

"Kwame," he supplied.

"Sorry, I'm terrible with names," said Marcia. She picked up her coat and book bag and waved to her new friends. Kwame watched her walk out the door of the pizzeria and look for the bus stop.

"Watch my backpack," said Kwame as he made his way out of the booth. "I want to make sure she gets on the right bus. Sometimes the bus number doesn't light up."

"Of course," said Cindy, struggling to keep her face serious. She watched Kwame as he hurried out the door. When she turned back to her friends, she found Sarah, Jennifer, April, and Tasha smiling and raising their eyebrows knowingly.

Two

Sarah stood in front of the three-way mirror next to the dressing room of the Ms. Tique store. She looked at the white denim pants she had tried on, then glanced at Tasha and Cindy. "What do you think? Too tight?" she asked them.

"No way," said Tasha. "You're just not used to wearing something that sexy."

Sarah looked at her reflection again and shook her head. "No," she said firmly, as she stepped off the raised platform. "Why should I spend good money on a pair of jeans that takes ten minutes to put on?"

"Girlfriend, you'd spend two hours squeezing into those pants if Dave said he liked them," Cindy teased.

Dave Hunter was Sarah's boyfriend. He lived across the street from the Gordons, and he and Sarah always hung out at each other's houses, doing homework, watching videos, or, best of all, doing absolutely nothing together.

"What Dave doesn't know won't hurt him," said Sarah, disappearing into the dressing room.

"What about you?" Tasha asked Cindy. "You got anything you want to wear for Mr. James?" After James Gethers had taken Cindy to the holiday dance last month, the two had dated several times. But Cindy hadn't mentioned him lately.

"James is trying to get out of that special reading class he's in," said Cindy.

"That's wonderful!" Sarah cried from behind the dressing room door.

"It is," Cindy agreed. "But it means he spends all of his afternoons at the tutoring lab. And that means he can't help his dad at the shop. Which means he has to help his dad on the weekends. Which means he doesn't have time to go out with me!"

"At least you know where your man is going after school," Tasha muttered.

Cindy rolled her eyes. "I can't believe Billy still hasn't told you anything!"

Tasha shook her head. "We talked on the phone for an hour last night, and I begged, pleaded, and threatened. No success."

Jennifer came out of the dressing room wearing a black tank top with a rose emblazoned on the front in a

14

shimmery gold fabric. "What do you think?" she asked Tasha and Cindy.

"Gorgeous!" said Cindy. She winced when she saw the price tag. "But way too expensive!"

"It's from Italy," Jennifer explained. She looked at her reflection and shook her head. "Not tight enough," she said finally.

Tasha ended up buying the white pants Sarah had rejected. "You'll be asking me to borrow them inside a week," she assured Sarah.

Sarah laughed. "You'll be asking me to cut you out of them!"

As they left the store, Cindy announced it was time to eat. They bought egg rolls at the Chinese carryout, and sat at a table next to the fountain in the middle of the mall's food court.

"Did anyone ever ask Marcia to come?" asked Jennifer, fanning her hot egg roll. "I don't think she knows about this mall."

"I called her this morning," said Sarah, "but she said she couldn't join us; she already had other plans."

"I think I know with who!" said Jennifer in a sing-song voice.

"Kwame?" said Cindy.

"Of course!" replied Jennifer. "Did you see how dazed he looked yesterday?"

"Yeah," said Tasha. "He was acting pretty strange—even for Kwame!" She laughed. "Love snuck up on him and hit him over the head!"

"That's not love," said Sarah. "Kwame's got a crush

on the girl, that's all." She pointed to an elderly black couple in front of the ice cream shop. "That's love," she said. The girls watched the couple walk off, licking cones and holding hands.

Jennifer looked at the old couple and wrinkled her nose. "They look kind of poor, don't they? Look at the man's pants."

"So what?" said Cindy. "I think they look cute."

"Would you rather have a career and make some money, or get married and wind up like that?" said Jennifer.

"Whoa, girl!" said Sarah. "You can be married *and* be successful."

"Yeah, that's what they tell you in *Essence* magazine," said Jennifer sarcastically. She picked up her napkin and rolled it back and forth across her knee. "My mom and dad didn't have any trouble until she started her design company," she said, gazing at the napkin. "I'm not saying it was the only reason they split up, but it didn't help."

"What about my parents?" said Sarah. "My dad is principal of Hamilton High, and my mom is a lawyer. They have a great relationship."

"They also have your grandmother helping out," Jennifer reminded her. "When she's not performing theater, Miss Essie is home, helping with the cooking or spending time with your sister." Jennifer pointed to the couple with the ice cream. "I hate to burst your bubble, Sarah, but love isn't always permanent. Take your couple over there. You can't assume those old

16

folks have been together from the start. They each might have been divorced one or two times."

"They're happy now," Sarah pointed out.

"Yeah, but they probably have kids who aren't," Jennifer muttered. "April would understand how I feel because her parents got divorced." She blinked hard and suddenly looked away.

"You can't let yourself get bitter," said Tasha, touching Jennifer's arm. "What happens if you find a man you're crazy about, and he asks you to marry him?" she asked softly. "Are you going to tell him, 'I love you, but I don't want to get married because I'm afraid we might get divorced'?"

Jennifer smiled as she wiped her eyes with the curled napkin. "It sounds stupid when you put it that way!" she admitted.

The four friends ate in silence. Finally, Cindy popped the last bit of egg roll into her mouth and slapped the table to get the others' attention. "I didn't come here to get married or start a career! I came to shop. Who's coming with me?"

Tasha and Sarah looked at Jennifer.

"Let's go, girlfriend!" Jennifer said, standing up.

They wandered around the mall for the rest of the afternoon, trying on blouses, spraying cologne testers, and walking in dozens of pairs of new shoes.

"Look who's here!" said Jennifer, pointing inside Worth's department store. They found Kwame leaning against a square pillar. He was reading a pamphlet and holding a large bag in his other hand.

"What's up?" he said, looking surprised.

"Kwame, what are you doing here?" Tasha asked him.

Marcia Dean appeared from behind a rack of shoes and waved.

"Whoa, girl, leave some shopping for later," said Tasha, looking at the enormous bag in Marcia's hand. "You're going to be in Madison a long time!"

Kwame took the bag from Marcia. "Let me hold that for you," he said.

Cindy pointed at Kwame. "Don't wear him out," she told Marcia. "Guys get tired of shopping pretty quick."

Marcia laughed. "Kwame's holding up fine. I just wish he didn't insist on carrying all my bags."

Kwame pretended to struggle with the weight. "They're not that heavy," he said through gritted teeth. The girls laughed.

"We were on our way to the second level," said Sarah. "Do you want to join us?" It looked as if Kwame was about to say yes, but Marcia nudged him.

"We still have other things to get around here," said Marcia. "Maybe we'll hook up with you later."

The girls watched them walk off. As soon as the couple was out of earshot, the girls burst into laughter.

"Did you see the look on Kwame's face? That boy is hooked," said Sarah. "I've never seen him so happy—not even when he's with you, Tasha."

"Yeah. I just hope he doesn't get hurt," Tasha answered as they rode the escalator to the second level of the mall.

"What do you mean by that, cuz?" Sarah asked.

"Marcia is new to the school," Tasha explained, "and right now, Kwame is her good friend. But once she starts knowing more people, she might leave him by the wayside."

"Who knows?" said Sarah. "Marcia might be as crazy about Kwame as he is about her."

"No, Tasha's right," said Jennifer. "A girl who looks like Marcia can have any guy she wants. Once she learns her way around and feels confident with herself, she'll wind up with one of the more popular guys."

Sarah thought this over. "She could do a lot worse than Kwame," she said.

"Kwame's a sophomore," said Tasha. "She's a junior. You think she's going to turn down a date with Derek Johnson or Tyler McPeak to stay with Kwame?"

"You and Jennifer make Kwame sound like a charity case," said Cindy.

"I'm just trying to look after a friend," Tasha insisted. "Now I'm wondering if introducing her to Kwame was such a good idea. He doesn't have much experience with romance, and I don't want to see him get hurt."

"Did you see how fast they disappeared?" said Sarah with a chuckle. "Those two wanted to be alone. The only 'hurt' Kwame's feeling right now is Cupid's arrow through his heart!"

"I hope so," said Tasha.

As they wandered around the second level of the mall, a redheaded girl approached them with a big smile. When they finally recognized the face, the four friends gasped.

"April! Is that you?" said Jennifer.

April smiled and ran her fingers through her newly tinted hair. "Well? What do you think?"

Up close, April's hair looked more orange than red.

"It's wild!" said Sarah truthfully.

"It changes your whole appearance," added Jennifer.

Tasha touched it lightly. "You had it permed, too."

"It's really... incredible," said Cindy.

"Thanks," said April. "It took me a while to work up the nerve to do it, but I got tired of being a blonde. Wait till Steve sees it—he'll flip!"

"He sure will," Tasha assured her. She tried to picture April's boyfriend's reaction. Steve Adams's own hair was naturally red. But if April had intended her new color to match his, the dye had fallen short.

"Of course, I'll have to get some clothes that look good with red hair," said April, almost to herself.

"Guess who we just saw together," said Cindy, her eyes gleaming.

"Marcia Dean and Kwame?" said April. Cindy's face fell. "I saw them heading toward the earring store. They're probably there right now," April said, falling in step with her friends. "Kwame was carrying these two huge bags. I thought he hated shopping."

"He does," Jennifer said, laughing. "But he sure loves to carry a pretty girl's bags!"

Sarah pointed at her cousin. "Tasha thinks Marcia

might drop Kwame when she gets to know more people at Murphy. Do you think that's true?"

April frowned. "It's possible," she said. "Kwame is so nice... Too nice, you know? I think girls like a guy with a little bit of an edge."

"Does Steve have an edge?" said Jennifer teasingly.

April blushed, which made her hair look even more orange. "You'd be surprised," she said. "He's not a big-time jock like Billy Simpson is, but he's not just a computer nerd, either."

"Really?" said Cindy. "What's he like alone?"

April raised her eyebrows meaningfully and smiled. "Different."

"Does he turn into a monster of passion?" asked Jennifer.

"No." April grinned. "But I do. And that's all I'm going to say." She stopped at a mirrored panel between two stores and looked at her hair from various angles. "What do you think? Now I'm not so sure I like it. Maybe I should have gotten a temporary dye."

"It's fabulous, April," said Sarah, patting her friend on the shoulder.

"It's hideous!" said Jennifer when the four of them were alone again. Through the glass doors, they saw Mrs. Wilson's car crossing the parking lot toward them.

"I know," said Sarah. "Maybe the color will tone down after she washes it."

"I'm worried about what Steve will say," said Tasha,

waving to Jennifer's mother. "He can be insensitive sometimes."

"Not insensitive," said Cindy, "just brutally honest."

"Sometimes it's the same thing," said Tasha.

PINE

Three

Tasha heard the tardy bell ring and cursed to herself. Slowly she inched forward on her hands and knees, looking under the desks and chairs of her English classroom for her gold pen. When she saw Ms. Bender approaching, she crawled out.

"Don't you have a class now, Tasha?" the teacher asked, glancing at the clock.

"This is my study period," said Tasha, dusting her knees. "Did someone turn in a pen to you? It's a gold-plated Fiehl ballpoint."

The teacher winced when she heard the expensive

brand name. "I'm afraid not. Are you sure you lost it during my class?"

"Positive," said Tasha. "I used it at my desk during the first half of class, but when we did the debate and everybody moved around, I guess I lost track of it."

"I'll keep looking," Ms. Bender promised. "In the meantime, I can lend you a plain old plastic pen for the rest of the day." She rummaged in her desk.

"Thanks anyway, but I have other pens in my backpack," said Tasha. Before she left, she took a final look at the floor. As she ran through the corridors, ignoring the scowls of the hall monitors, Tasha felt her temper rising. Losing things made her feel stupid, and she hated feeling stupid.

She slipped into the science lab, where she liked to spend her study period. In the back of the classroom, she spied Jack Hoy, a student in her English class.

"What's up?" Jack whispered when Tasha took the seat next to his.

Tasha told him about the missing pen. "I'm starting to think one of the debaters on your team used it for a minute, then automatically stuck it in his pocket."

Jack frowned. "Maybe," he said. "But I was the official note-taker for our team. Nobody else needed a pen at that time."

"I wish I had been note-taker for my team," Tasha muttered.

"I'm sure it'll turn up," said Jack. "In the meantime, if you need to borrow a pen—" But Tasha was already shaking her head.

24

At the end of the day, Tasha went to the main office to look through the Lost and Found box. She rummaged through a pile of old wool caps and unmatched mittens. She made a face when she saw the bottom of the box: four combs, a cracked ruler, a cheap digital watch with no wristband—and no pens.

Walking out of the main office, Tasha spied Amanda Dennis walking toward the front doors. Amanda was a dancer, as well as a member of the Murphy High pep squad. The leader of the squad, Debby Barnes, didn't like the 18 Pine St. friends, and encouraged Amanda and the other cheerleaders to make life difficult for them, even though Tasha and her friends always found a way to pay them back.

Amanda had been on Jack Hoy's debating team, too. It occurred to Tasha that Amanda might have taken the pen just to cause trouble. If Debby Barnes liked to pull mean stunts, a friend of Debby's might do so as well, she reasoned. Tasha ran up to the cheerleader.

"I need to talk to you for a minute," Tasha said.

Amanda seemed surprised to hear Tasha talking to her. She gave Tasha a chilly stare. "I'm in a hurry," she said.

Tasha ignored the look. "Did you see a gold pen on my desk in Ms. Bender's class today?"

"Yes, I did," said Amanda calmly.

"Did you see someone take it?"

"No, I did not," said Amanda, arching an eyebrow.

Linda Plunkett, another member of the pep squad, saw the two girls talking and approached them.

25

"This girl's calling me a thief," said Amanda. Linda scowled.

"I didn't call you that," Tasha replied hotly. "I just asked you a question."

"And I answered it!" said Amanda. The two girls glowered at Tasha and then brushed past her.

"If I find out you're lying, you'll be sorry," Tasha called after them. The pep squad girls laughed at her threat.

As Tasha watched them leave, she recalled what her grandmother had said the night she'd taught Tasha to play hearts. "If you can't count cards, learn to read faces." Tasha had kept her eyes on Amanda's face, looking for signs of nervousness or forced calm, but she had found none. "If she did lie, she was very cool about it," Tasha muttered to herself.

"I'll help you look around tomorrow," said Sarah as they rode the bus home. "We'll put a notice on the activities bulletin board about it."

Tasha stared at the snow-coated trees through the dirty bus window. "We'll try the notices, but I think someone would have turned it in by now. My guess is somebody stole it."

"Would it cost a lot to replace?" Cindy asked.

"It's not a priceless antique," said Tasha with a sigh. "But it was my grandmother's present, and I don't want her to know I lost it less than a month after she gave it to me."

Sarah pulled a wire-bound notebook from her backpack and tore a sheet out. She wrote "Classmates Who Might Steal" on the top and handed the paper to Tasha.

Tasha wrote down Denny and Van, two guys who were always getting in trouble with Ms. Bender. Then she remembered that they had been on her debating team, and she crossed the names out. "I can't think of anyone else," she told her friends. "I talked to Amanda after school, and I'm pretty sure she didn't do it."

"Why don't you make a list of everyone on the other debating team?" Sarah suggested.

Tasha closed her eyes and pictured the students: Jack Hoy, Brian Wu, Lisa Marks, Damon Beraud, Donna Hagood, Amanda Dennis, and Marcia Dean. "What about Marcia?" she said aloud.

"You'd better have some proof before you accuse her," said Cindy, grinning. "She might sic Kwame on you!" She leaned closer to the Gordon cousins. "She was at his house last night, you know," she said in a low voice.

"Who told you that?" said Sarah.

"I called him at nine-thirty," replied Cindy. "Actually, the reason I called was to ask him about his thing with Marcia!"

Sarah grinned. "I don't know who's worse when it comes to gossip, you or April!"

"It's not gossip, it's concern," said Cindy piously.

"Did you see them at lunch today, sitting alone together at that other table?" Sarah asked. "Kwame didn't even look up when Steve called him. When you don't pay attention to your best friend anymore, you are hopelessly in love."

"Speaking of Steve," Cindy interrupted, "do you think he knows that April changed her hair color? April didn't come to school today, you know."

"I don't think he saw it over the weekend, or he would have mentioned it," said Tasha. "I would be very surprised if Steve wound up liking April as a red-head."

"You mean orangehead!" said a sophomore boy in the seat in front of theirs. He turned around to face the girls. "I saw April at the mall on Saturday. That hair ain't red, it's pumpkin-colored."

Tasha leaned forward in her seat and glowered at the boy. "Watch what you say," she warned. "April is a friend of mine, you hear?"

Sarah and Cindy stared coldly at him as well. The boy's smirk dimmed, and he mumbled an apology as he shrank back into his seat.

"He's right, though," Sarah whispered. "I'm hoping the color faded a little bit."

"Ain't that much fading in the world!" said Cindy, shaking her head.

When the Gordon cousins got home, they headed straight for the kitchen. Sarah poured herself a bowl of cereal, while Tasha took an apple from the fruit basket. "By the way, Sarah," Tasha said as she washed the apple, "thanks for not saying it."

"Saying what?" said Sarah, looking up from her cereal.

"That I shouldn't have taken an expensive pen to

school, where it could get stolen," said Tasha. "You kept yours at home where it was safe."

"It hadn't even entered my mind, cuz," said Sarah.

"Still," said Tasha through a mouthful of apple "if I had kept it here, I'd still have it."

"You don't really know that it was stolen," Sarah pointed out. "What if it dropped on the floor and got kicked under a radiator or something?"

"No," said Tasha. "I looked all over Ms. Bender's room." She sighed loudly. "Miss Essie will think I'm some kind of fool to lose it so soon."

"Why don't we go out this weekend to buy a replacement, so Miss Essie doesn't find out?" Sarah asked. "I'll lend you some money, if you need it."

Tasha smiled. "Thanks, but no thanks. Nobody steals from Tasha Gordon and gets away with it. If I find out who took it—" She held up the apple and took a huge bite from it. "Just like that," she told her cousin.

18 PINE

Four

By noon the next day, Tasha's pen was still missing. No one had responded to the sign she had taped onto the activities bulletin board, even after she wrote "Reward for its return" at the bottom of the notice.

As she walked toward the cafeteria, Tasha suddenly felt a pair of arms squeezing her around the middle. Billy Simpson spun her once and set her down again. Tasha turned to scowl at him, but her expression softened when she saw his handsome, wide-set eyes and impish grin.

"What's up?" said Billy in a raspy voice.

"Not much, stranger," Tasha replied. "I haven't seen you much lately."

"I know," he said. "I've been busy—busier than a one-legged man in a butt-kicking contest!"

"You're a mess," said Tasha, laughing. "So, what are you going to do to make up for the fact that you didn't take me out last Friday?"

Billy placed his hand over his heart. "I'll give you cars, jewels, furs, and two tickets for Def Cru 2 next time they're in town," he vowed.

"I'll settle for a ride in that car of yours this afternoon." Tasha grinned.

Billy hesitated. "I'm kind of tied up these days after school," he said.

"So what's her name?" Tasha asked.

"It's nothing like that. I know better than to cheat on you! Like I told you," Billy added, "I have a job now." His voice faded as he spoke, and he cleared his throat loudly.

"What's up with that throat of yours?" said Tasha. "Do you scream all day at this job?"

"I... I don't want to talk about it, okay? Please?"

Tasha stopped in the middle of the hallway. "Billy, I'm your girlfriend, aren't I? I know things about you that nobody else knows. You know things about me that not even Sarah knows about."

"That's true," said Billy. "And if I ever decide to tell anyone, you'll be the first to know."

"If I guess, will you tell me if I'm right?" asked Tasha.

Billy thought about it for a moment, then agreed.

"Pizza delivery? Telemarketing? Custodian? Baby-sitting? Envelope stuffing? Construction? Painting? Housecleaning? Data entry? Burger flipper? Veterinarian's assistant?"

Billy smiled and shook his head each time.

"How would you like it if I kept secrets from you?" demanded Tasha.

"I'd hate it," said Billy. "But then I'd say to myself, 'There must be a reason she's not telling me,' and I'd stop asking about it."

Tasha glared at him. "Well, I'm not going to stop asking."

Suddenly Billy laughed. "If my football team were this stubborn, we'd have made the state finals!" But Tasha was not amused. They walked the rest of the way to the cafeteria in silence. When Billy pulled out a chair for Tasha, she ignored it and sat next to José Melendez at the other end of the table.

When Kwame and Steve Adams came to the table, the two of them were so engrossed in their conversation that they didn't greet the others. Steve wore a baggy sweater and a loose pair of khaki slacks that made him look even thinner than he was. He had gotten a haircut over the holidays, but his red hair still looked unkempt. He combed it absently with his fingers as he and Kwame argued.

"There's no way the Belgian Ogre could beat Fabulous Fishman," Steve insisted. "Don's had the world wrestling title for three years!"

"He's never wrestled anyone like the Ogre before," Kwame countered. "Did you see what the

Ogre did to Fabulous Fishman?"

Steve lifted the pudding cup from his lunch tray. "A week of lunch desserts says Don takes him down."

"For heaven's sake, listen to you," said Jennifer to the two of them. "How can you take that world wrestling seriously? It's fake! Those people aren't really wrestling!"

Steve and Kwame stared at Jennifer as if she was missing the point. "We know it's rigged," said Steve. "But we don't know which way it's rigged."

Kwame picked up his pudding cup. "The match is on Saturday. We'll watch it at my place."

"Fine," said Steve, smiling. "It'll save you a *looong* walk home!" He looked around the cafeteria, then turned to his other friends. "Is April out of school today again?"

Tasha and the other girls traded looks.

"She's here today," said Kwame. He shook his head in disbelief. "I saw her in French class, and boy does she look—" He stopped as soon as he felt Jennifer's kick to his shins.

"Hey, kids!" said April, appearing from behind Steve.

Steve turned around, smiling. Then his head snapped back in shock. "April, your hair!" he wailed.

"Do you like it?" said April.

Steve glared at the rest of the table. "Did you guys put her up to this?" he whispered.

The girls put their hands over their hearts and solemnly shook their heads.

34

April set her book bag down and tousled Steve's hair. "Now we're both redheads," she said. Her smile faded as she looked at her boyfriend. "You don't like it, do you?"

"Well—I—" Steve stammered. He saw that April was getting upset. "I wasn't ready for it. It's...really punk-looking," he said with a brave smile. He pulled out the chair next to him and offered it to her.

"Do you think it looks weird?" April demanded.

"Steve didn't say that," said Kwame.

"I told you, I just wasn't used to it," said Steve. "You know how much I like redheads."

"Better not like them too much," said April. "I might get tired of this and change back."

"Oh, I like blondes, too!" said Steve quickly.

"Hi, everybody," said Marcia, sitting next to Kwame. She rummaged through her backpack and pulled out a small bag. Inside were a pair of copper-colored earrings. She handed them to April. "I got these at a thrift store. They'd go great with your new look."

"They're pretty," April agreed, pulling out her earrings and inserting the new ones. "Thanks."

"Yuck." José Melendez shuddered. "I can't stand to see a woman putting on earrings," he said. "Driving a piece of metal through your flesh!"

"It doesn't hurt, José," said Jennifer. "It only hurts a little when you first get them pierced."

"Unless the ear gets infected," Cindy pointed out. "Then the lobe swells up—"

Billy cleared his throat loudly. "Do you mind, Cindy?" he said, holding a soup spoon in midair. "I'm trying to eat over here!"

Marcia tugged on Kwame's shoulder. "Let's go to that other table, where we can be alone," she said. Kwame got up to follow her.

"Hey, where are you two going?" said April.

"Kwame and I have some things to talk about," said Marcia. The guys at the table whooped at that, and Kwame frowned at them.

"Why did you tell April those earrings came from a thrift store?" Kwame asked Marcia when the two of them were alone. "I thought you got them at that earring boutique in the mall."

"I did," said Marcia. "But April might feel bad accepting an expensive pair of earrings from me. She might feel she has to repay me or something. This way, it takes the pressure off."

"Good thinking," said Kwame admiringly. "You're so considerate." He glanced back at the table where his friends sat. "I think those earrings made April feel a lot better about her hair, too."

Marcia smiled and looked down at her food. "I want to get started on the right foot with your friends," she said. "My dad moves around a lot in his job and it was hard for me to make friends with the kids in Philadelphia. Everyone knew each other from their junior high schools, and I was the new kid. I hated that."

"You've already made plenty of friends here," Kwame assured her. "Everybody loves you."

Especially me, he thought.

"You're sweet, Kwame," said Marcia. "I think your friends do like me, but sometimes I see Jennifer looking at me funny." Kwame gave her a surprised look. "Not all the time," Marcia added quickly, "just once in a while."

"Give her some time to get used to you," said Kwame. "But if she keeps it up, tell me about it, and I'll set her straight!"

Tasha watched Billy place his empty lunch tray on the conveyor belt that led to the cafeteria dishwasher. "I'm going to hire me a detective," she said to her friends.

"Too bad Kwame is tied up," said Jennifer. "Remember how he helped us find the guy who ran into my mom's car?"

"I hate to admit it, Tasha, but I'm starting to get a little curious about Billy myself," Sarah told her cousin. "I mean, if Billy is just going to a job, what's the big deal? Why can't he just tell us about it?"

"Maybe it's something really embarrassing," said Cindy. "My uncle once got paid to take these psychological tests at a college, and he didn't tell anyone for years."

"It could be secret work for the government," chimed in Robert Thornton in a deep voice. He was the class clown, and he was always ready to turn his friends into an audience for his jokes. "He could be one of those high school cops, like on TV! Maybe his

37

front teeth are really a microphone, so he smiles, then waits for us to talk about a big drug shipment—"

"Thanks, Robert," said Tasha wearily, "but I'm serious."

"I've got it," said José. "Billy is rehearsing a play. That's why he always leaves right after school, and the reason he's hoarse is that the part calls for a lot of yelling."

"Billy wouldn't be caught dead on a stage," said Tasha, shaking her head. Something Robert had mentioned had filled her with dread. "Do you think it could be drugs? Maybe he's inhaling something that's affecting his throat?"

"He's an athlete," Sarah reminded her. "And he's not an idiot. He wouldn't do any of that junk."

"Then what is that boy doing?" said Tasha, looking around the table. But her friends were as mystified as she was.

Five

After school, Kwame wanted to go to 18 Pine to see his friends. But Marcia insisted they go to the Westcove Mall. Kwame quickly decided it wasn't worth arguing over. He could go to 18 Pine any day.

The two largest earring stores were located at opposite ends of the mall. A Fair Earring! was near Worth's department store. When Kwame and Marcia walked into the boutique, there were no customers in the place.

Marcia wandered around the store aisles with a sour expression on her face. "Nothing but junk in here!" she whispered. "Let's go to the other one."

The two made their way to Maya, a store that sold South American goods. Kwame pointed to the sign as they went in. "The Mayan civilization lived in what is now Central America and Mexico," he told Marcia. "But this store sells things from Ecuador, Argentina, and Colombia, and they're in South America. I wonder if anyone has ever noticed." He glanced at Marcia, who was scanning the racks of jewelry as she nodded politely. Kwame felt his face getting warm. She thinks you're showing off, said a voice inside him.

Kwame remembered feeling the same way on their shopping trip over the weekend. When he'd told her about the bayonet he was planning to buy and its importance as a weapon of the Revolutionary War, he had sensed that Marcia was only listening to be nice. I wasn't trying to show off or anything, he told himself. Do I always sound like a nerd when I'm talking about the things that interest me?

Maya was crowded that afternoon. The yellow Sale signs had attracted many shoppers to the store. A group of children crowded next to a birdcage in the back, where a toucan with a beak like a banana jumped nervously from perch to perch. Only one salesman seemed to be on the shop floor, while a cashier rang up purchases for a long line of customers.

Kwame stole a look at Marcia, who was wearing torn jeans and her brother's oversize Bulls jacket. Her hair was combed back on the sides. She's so beautiful, Kwame thought for the hundredth time since he'd met her.

He touched his stomach self-consciously. He had never really cared about his looks, but now he found himself wishing he had a hard, bulky body like Billy, or the lean, muscled grace of a basketball player like Dave Hunter. From now on, no more junk food, he told himself.

He followed Marcia as she wound her way between display tables piled high with handwoven shirts, canvas trousers, and colorful bandannas. One wall was devoted to earrings, and Marcia pointed it out to Kwame.

"Could you do me a favor?" she asked, flashing her gray eyes at him. "I saw a pair of earrings the last time we were here—blue stones on a silver back. Do you mind looking for them while I check out this bargain bin?"

"No problem," said Kwame. He walked to the wall and began to search. Until he'd met Marcia, he had never given jewelry much thought. He was surprised at the variety of styles and patterns there were. I've been noticing a lot of new things since Marcia came into my life, he thought happily. He scanned the rows of earrings from right to left, then from top to bottom. When he found two pairs that fit Marcia's description, he reached up to pull them down.

"Can I help you with something?"

Kwame jumped. It was the salesman manning the floor—a short, middle-aged white man with a gray mustache and rimless glasses. Kwame pointed out the pairs he wanted, and the man took them down for him. I could have done that myself, Kwame thought. He noticed with some irritation that Rimless Glasses was letting the women take down the earrings themselves. Obviously this guy was afraid Kwame would try to steal something.

Kwame took the earrings to Marcia, who was hunched over a counter between two middle-aged women. He tapped her shoulder and showed her the earrings. Marcia shook her head.

"Those aren't the ones I saw here the other day," she said. "Too bad, because my mom would have loved them."

"She wouldn't like either of these pairs?" Kwame asked.

"Well, she might like these," said Marcia, pointing to his left hand. She looked at the back of the card and her face fell. "They're ten dollars too much."

Kwame returned to the earring wall. He couldn't stand to see Marcia look so disappointed. Impulsively he replaced one pair and took the other to the cash register, making sure Marcia wasn't watching. He couldn't wait to surprise her.

"Cash or credit?" asked the tired cashier.

"Cash," said Kwame. "The bayonet will have to wait," he mumbled to himself.

While the woman rang up the earrings, Kwame looked around the store. He noticed he was the only male in the place, besides Mr. Rimless Glasses. The middle-aged salesman was now dusting a group of wooden statues on a counter. The man was looking directly at him, and Kwame quickly looked away.

After his purchase, Kwame counted his change and

sighed. There was not enough money left to take Marcia to the movies, as he'd planned.

"Find anything?" he asked her once they were outside the store.

"Not much," said Marcia. "Those old ladies really cleaned the place out." She spied an ice cream store and grabbed Kwame by the arm. "Ooh, ice cream," she said in a childlike voice.

Kwame tapped his pockets and did some quick calculating. "Come on, I'll treat you."

They sat on a bench with their ice cream cones and watched the shoppers walk by.

"I had a dream about you," Marcia told him.

"Really?" Kwame was flattered. "What did I do? Was it a good dream or a nightmare?"

"You and I were at a party, dancing," she said. "We even won a dance contest. Then this guy tried to take me away from you, but you challenged him to a duel."

"A duel!"

"Yes," said Marcia, laughing. "You even gave him a sword. It was like *The Three Musketeers*."

"Let that be a lesson to anyone who tries to mess with you," said Kwame, puffing out his chest. "Uh, did I win?"

"You won," said Marcia.

Kwame put his arm around her shoulder and pulled her close.

"Oh, I almost forgot," he said when they'd finished their ice cream. He pulled out the bag with the earrings and put it in her hand. "For your mother."

43

"Kwame!" Marcia exclaimed. She reached into the bag and pulled out the earrings. "They're more beautiful than I first thought," she said, touching them delicately.

"I know they're not the ones your mother wanted," said Kwame, "but maybe she'll like them."

"She'll love them," Marcia promised him. "And if she doesn't, I will! I still can't believe you bought them." She gave him a suspicious grin. "Or did you boost them?"

"'Boost?'" said Kwame.

"You know, steal," said Marcia. "I didn't take you for the type."

Kwame fumbled in his pocket for the receipt. "I didn't 'boost' them. What kind of guy do you think I am?"

"I was just kidding, silly," said Marcia. She reached into the pocket of her oversize jacket and pulled out an orange and blue cloth band.

"What's this?" said Kwame.

"It's from Guatemala," said Marcia. "It's a friendship band. I got it for you at Maya." She put the cloth band in Kwame's hand.

"I'll never take it off," he promised.

She grazed his cheek with her lips and he could feel her breath in soft puffs against his skin. Eagerly he turned toward her. As they kissed in the middle of the mall, Kwame forgot about the passersby, the bayonet, and even about breathing.

When she pulled away, Marcia gave him a shy

smile. "Let me help you with that," she said, taking the friendship band from his damp hand and tying it onto his wrist. "There's more where that came from."

"You don't have to buy me anything else," said Kwame.

"I was talking about the kiss," Marcia whispered in his ear.

Kwame grinned, but remained silent. Say something, you idiot! he told himself.

He pointed at the blue earrings in Marcia's hand. "It's funny that you mentioned stealing. That guy in Maya thought I was going to take those."

Marcia frowned. "He probably saw a young black man and decided automatically that you were a criminal."

"That's exactly what I thought," Kwame replied. "He kept his eye on me the entire time we were in there."

Marcia stood up quickly and pulled Kwame by the wrist. "Let's go back there and tell that idiot off."

"No, really!" said Kwame, pulling back his hand. "Let's not go back there, okay? I can't prove he was prejudiced—it's just a feeling I had."

"That kind of thing happened to me in Philly," said Marcia, scowling. "My friends and I were in a record store, and I caught the guy behind the counter nodding his head in my direction. All my friends were white, so he didn't care about them. Anyway, after the counterman nodded, I suddenly noticed a store lady following me wherever I went. Finally, I turned to the lady and

45

said, 'I don't need any help, thank you.' The lady gave me this suspicious look and said, 'Well, I'll be right here if you do.'"

Kwame shook his head.

"A hundred white girls in the store, and she had to pick on me!" said Marcia plaintively. "I never went back there again. Then my friends and I organized a boycott of the place in our school."

"Good for you!" cried Kwame. That was the kind of action he liked to hear about. If people didn't do anything, things would always be the same. Admiration for Marcia welled inside him. He wished he could hop a plane to Philadelphia and confront the woman who had suspected his girlfriend. With the Musketeer sword he had wielded in Marcia's dream, he would see to it that the entire store apologized.

"Kwame, are you all right?"

"Huh? Yeah, I'm okay," said Kwame, snapping out of his daydream. I'm hopelessly in love with you, but I'm okay.

They wandered through Worth's and other mall stores, stopping wherever anything caught their eye.

"Ooh, popcorn!" said Marcia when she saw a vendor filling a bag for a customer.

Kwame cursed softly. "I'm sorry, Marcia, I'm tapped out."

"That's okay," said Marcia, reaching into her pocketbook. "We'll grab a small box for the bus ride home." She stopped abruptly and pointed to a figure that was striding into the video arcade. "Hey, isn't that

46

one of your friends?" she asked.

Kwame followed her gaze and saw Steve disappearing into the game room. He knew his friend was going in just to play Open Season. It was Kwame and Steve's favorite game, but Steve was the master of it. He consistently beat the highest score posted on the machine. Often he would let younger kids take his turn, once he had accumulated enough extra duck hunters.

"Let's go say hi," said Kwame, hoping to get a turn at the machine.

Marcia stood still. "I can't; I have to get going," she said. "My dad is going to kill me as it is."

"Can't have that," said Kwame with a smile.

"I know it sounds silly, but I'm still a little unsure of the bus route," said Marcia shyly. "Would you mind riding with me to my stop?"

Marcia lived seven stops past Kwame's house. *I'll have to walk back in the slush for at least a half mile,* he realized. But instead of saying anything, he put his arm around her and kissed her quickly on the cheek.

"Of course I'll go to your stop with you," he said. "What are Musketeers for?"

Six

On Wednesday after school, the gang met at 18 Pine St. When Steve placed the basket of steak fries in the middle of the table, Kwame forced himself to keep his hands at his sides. He watched enviously as Dave, Sarah, Tasha, and Jennifer reached into it at once. The smell of fried potatoes reached Kwame's nose, and he swallowed hard as he eyed them longingly. Be strong, he told himself.

During the ride home from the mall the evening before, Marcia had poked Kwame's stomach playfully. He kept remembering the little jab as he walked the half mile to his house. He had touched his soft stomach with disgust, and he vowed to get in better shape. He

49

still ached from the fifteen sit-ups he had done the minute he had come home.

In the back booth of 18 Pine St., he stared at the steak fries defiantly. It was as if they were there to test his willpower, and he wasn't going to give in.

Steve glanced around the pizzeria for a sign of April, then looked back at his friends. "Okay. Did somebody put April up to it?" he asked.

"We were just as surprised as you were," said Dave as he dragged a steak fry through a puddle of ketchup. He put his arm around Sarah's shoulder and grinned. "I don't think April's hair is that bad. I've been trying to get Sarah here to be a blonde, but she won't go for it."

"Black," said Sarah, giving him a playful shove. "Take it or leave it!"

"This morning I almost got into a fight with a guy who made a joke about her," Steve muttered. "The thing that bothered me most about it was that he was right."

"Does it matter what she looks like?" asked Jennifer. "We all like April for who she is. Isn't her personality the most important thing?"

"I hate to admit it, Jennifer, but orange hair matters," said Steve. He looked at each of his friends. "Am I the only one who thinks she looked better in her natural hair color?"

"I agree with you, Steve. She looked better before," said Sarah. "But if we say something now, we'll hurt her feelings. What do you think?" she said, turning to Kwame.

"Huh?" said Kwame, snapping out of a daydream. "What are we talking about?"

"We were talking about how you've been in orbit the past week!" Tasha teased. "How come you're not off with Marcia? Is she sick today or something?"

"She's supposed to be here," Kwame replied. He pointed to the orange and blue cloth band on his wrist. "Did I show you what she gave me?"

"Only a million times at lunch!" said Jennifer.

Kwame ignored her. "It's a friendship band, and a good-luck charm," he told them.

"Maybe you should lend it to the Belgian Ogre," said Steve. "He's going to need it against Fabulous Don!"

Kwame suddenly remembered the bet he had with Steve. "I meant to tell you. I can't see the match with you this Saturday," he said. "Something came up."

"That's cool," said Steve. But Kwame could see he was disappointed. "Still want to go through with the bet?" Steve asked.

"Even if I win, you can have my desserts," said Kwame, poking Steve's thin shoulder. "You need 'em."

"I can't believe what I just heard!" Jennifer said, shaking her head. "Kwame turned down a wrestling match and a week of extra desserts right before my very eyes. Man, have you changed!"

Kwame grinned.

"And here comes the reason why," said Tasha, pointing to the street outside.

Marcia waved to the group when she saw them through the large plate-glass window at the front of the pizzeria. She stopped at the counter to order a slice of pizza before joining them. Extra cheese, Kwame noticed as he pulled out a chair for her.

Marcia shook her head. "I have to talk to you alone," she whispered to him. As Kwame stood up, she turned to the others. "I had my first encounter with the vice-principal today," she announced.

"Uh-oh, what happened?" asked Jennifer.

"He thought I was smoking in the girls' bathroom," said Marcia, rolling her eyes. "I guess you could smell all the tobacco smoke in there out in the hallway, because he was waiting outside the door. I was the first one to leave so he nabbed me."

"Mr. Schlesinger has a nose like a bloodhound!" said Dave.

"The place already reeked of smoke when I went in there, and that's what I told him," said Marcia. "But I could tell he didn't really believe me."

"Don't worry," said Jennifer. "He's just trying to intimidate you. He won't actually scream at you until he catches you red-handed."

There was a pause as Marcia pursed her lips and looked straight into Jennifer's eyes. "What do you mean, 'until he catches me red-handed'? I told you I wasn't the one who was smoking."

"I didn't mean you personally," said Jennifer, taken aback by Marcia's flare of temper. "I meant to say that Schlesinger won't scream at *anyone* until he catches

52

him or her in the act."

"Oh, I see," said Marcia. She smiled apologetically at Jennifer, then said, "Kwame and I will be right back."

Kwame was glad she chose a table by the windows. Any Murphy High guys walking past would glance at the attractive girl, then turn to see who she was with.

"You can have some," said Marcia when she caught Kwame looking at her slice of pizza.

"No, thanks," said Kwame brightly. "I'm not hungry." Just then his stomach growled long and loud. The sound reminded Kwame of the seals in the Madison aquarium. His face grew hot as Marcia gave him a startled look.

"Are you sure?" said Marcia, holding the slice in front of her. "There's plenty here."

"Really, I'm fine," said Kwame with a nervous laugh. But the seals in his stomach cried out again. The noise was so loud that two college girls at a nearby table turned to look at him.

"Well, maybe one bite," said Kwame miserably. He took a big bite and chewed it as slowly as he could. "What did you want to talk about?" he asked.

Marcia reached into her backpack and pulled out a pad of paper. "I want you to take a personality quiz. My girlfriends and I used to do this back in Philly. Just draw a picture of a woman using only squares, circles, or triangles—any combination of them, but only using ten."

Kwame was a little surprised that she'd pulled him

away from the others for this, but the chance to be alone with her was more than he could resist.

"What will it tell me about my personality?" he asked.

Marcia smiled at him and handed him a pen. "I'll tell you after you draw the picture."

Jennifer watched Kwame and Marcia huddling at the table up front. "Did you see how angry Marcia got when she thought I was accusing her of smoking?" she asked her friends.

"I don't know why she got so upset," said Steve. "Everybody knew what you meant."

"She's touchy, all right," said Tasha. She looked at Marcia, then at Kwame, who was concentrating on a sheet of paper in front of him. She watched as he drew on it, then absently tapped his cheek with his pen.

Tasha's jaw dropped. She grabbed Jennifer's arm and made her look at the other table. "Kwame has my pen!" she cried.

"Are you sure?" said Jennifer. "Maybe it's one just like it." She followed Tasha, who walked to the counter in front of the cash register. Marcia's back was to them, and Tasha carefully observed Kwame as he wrote.

"Thin, gold-colored, a black band on the tip," murmured Tasha. "That's it, all right."

"How could Kwame have taken your pen?" Jennifer asked.

"He didn't, but Marcia did. She's in my English class," Tasha reminded her. "Do me a favor, Jennifer, and distract Kwame for a minute."

The two girls approached the couple's table. "Excuse me, Kwame, could I talk to you? It's very important." Jennifer smiled apologetically at Marcia. "I have to borrow him for a minute," she told the other girl.

Kwame glanced at Marcia.

"We're in the middle of something," Marcia said haughtily. "Can it wait a few minutes?"

"No, it can't," said Jennifer, pulling Kwame up by the arm. As Kwame and Jennifer moved away, Tasha reached for the pen he had set down. But Marcia's hand was much faster. She grabbed it before Tasha could.

"I think that's my pen." said Tasha, trying to control her temper.

"This pen is mine." Marcia gave Tasha an icy stare. "I heard you lost your pen, but this one ain't yours."

"Did you find it in English class?" asked Tasha, sitting in Kwame's seat.

"No," said Marcia, unzipping her book bag and dropping the pen inside. "I got it for Christmas from my grandmother."

"You didn't mention it before," said Tasha. "First time you came to 18 Pine, we were talking about gifts, remember? You said your grandmother got you a sweater."

Marcia narrowed her eyes. "I've got two grandmothers," she said. "And I don't appreciate being called a thief!" she added loudly.

At that Kwame looked up and quickly returned to the table.

"What's going on?" he asked.

"You tell me, Kwame," said Marcia, still looking at Tasha. "Is this how you treat all the new kids at Murphy, Tasha? I thought you were my friend!"

Tasha stood up. "And I thought you were mine!" she shot back. "Someone took my Fiehl pen in English class, and now one of those classmates is walking around with one just like it. I have a right to be suspicious."

"Do you have proof, Tasha?" Kwame asked quietly. Tasha's outburst was typical of her quick temper, and he expected her to calm down in a moment. Steve, Dave, and Sarah were attracted by the commotion and joined the others at the front of the pizzeria.

"You and your friends can't scare me," said Marcia, whose eyes were now brimming with tears.

"Just give me back my pen," said Tasha.

"Hey, cuz, maybe it really is her pen," said Sarah.

Tasha turned to her cousin. "Whose side are you on?"

"Tasha has a right to be suspicious," said Jennifer.

"You need proof! Get proof or leave her alone," said Kwame, trying to control his own temper.

A pair of flour-dusted hands pushed through the crowd. Mr. Harris, the owner of the pizzeria, stood before them. He glared at them until they all quieted down. "Do you mind?" he said. "I'm trying to run a business! Everyone sit down, or take it outside."

Tasha and Sarah mumbled an apology and then sat down. But Marcia picked up her coat and backpack and headed for the door. Kwame watched her walk out, then turned to his friends. No one spoke.

"I think you should apologize to her," Kwame told Tasha quietly.

"Apologize?" said Tasha. "What should I say, 'I'm sorry you stole from me'?"

"Just apologize for losing your temper," said Kwame. "Then we can talk about this whole stealing thing." He looked out the window and watched Marcia cross the street toward the bus stop. He turned to Tasha again. "Do it for me."

"I'm sorry, Kwame," said Tasha, shaking her head. "But I don't feel I did anything wrong."

"You insulted my girlfriend," he replied angrily. Without another word, Kwame picked up his coat and headed for the door.

"Kwame, where are you going, man?" Dave asked.

"Yeah, let's talk this over," said Steve.

But Kwame did not turn back. The wind stung his face as he zipped up his coat. At the bus stop he found Marcia wiping her eyes on her mittens. "Do you have to go home right away?" he asked.

"I think I'd better," said Marcia. "And I'd like to be alone."

To Kwame, the sky seemed to darken as she said it. "I believe you about the pen," he said.

"You're just being nice," said Marcia, looking at the sidewalk. "Why don't you go back to your friends?"

"I'm with one of them right now," he replied. Marcia looked up at him. She put her head on his shoulder, and Kwame gave her a slow, rocking hug.

"You know what?" said Marcia, moments later.

"What?" said Kwame.

She smiled at him. "I don't deserve someone as nice as you," she said, poking him affectionately.

Kwame smiled. This time he was ready for the poke, and he clenched his stomach muscles.

Seven

Tasha found her aunt in the attic.

"Back here," said Mrs. Gordon from behind a dusty room divider. Tasha followed the voice and saw that her aunt was sorting piles of old dishes. "I volunteered for a charity auction," Mrs. Gordon explained. She wiped her hands on her jeans and shook her head at the mess around her. "I should have offered to donate money instead of time," she said wearily. "Although heaven knows, there never seems to be enough of either one."

"Not much honesty in the world either," said Tasha,

sitting on a pile of old newspapers. She told her aunt what had happened at 18 Pine St. "I'm positive Marcia took that pen," she added. "But I just can't prove it. What should I do?"

Mrs. Gordon handed Tasha a stack of old *National Geographic* magazines and motioned for her to put them by the attic door. "If you were one of my law clients, I would have to advise you to drop the case," she said.

"But then she gets away with it!" Tasha cried.

"Did anyone see this girl take the property?" asked Mrs. Gordon. "Were there any marks on it that could identify the property as yours?"

"No," said Tasha to both questions.

"In our justice system, the burden of proof is on the accuser," said Mrs. Gordon. "There are still some countries where the citizens are guilty until they can prove they're innocent. But the U.S. isn't like that, thank goodness." She gave Tasha a sympathetic look. "I know this must be very frustrating for you."

"It's not just the pen," Tasha said glumly. She ran a finger along the edge of a dusty rocking chair. "I feel like whoever took it was out to get me personally!"

"I know what you mean." Mrs. Gordon nodded. "That's how many crime victims feel. When a thief takes something that belongs to you, it's natural to feel paranoid or uneasy. You wonder if someone is out for revenge. But that's usually not the case. A thief just wants the objects you own—it has nothing to do with you personally."

"Since I don't have proof, are you saying I should just forget about it?" asked Tasha.

"No, don't forget about it," her aunt told her. "But do something to prevent it from happening again. Mark your valuables. If marked objects are stolen, then turn up somewhere, you can prove they're yours."

Tasha thanked her aunt and returned to her room. She removed her watch from her wrist. With a steel hatpin from her sewing box, she carefully scratched "TG" on the back plate. It took a long time to run a groove into the metal, but when she was finished, the initials stood out boldly. She almost jabbed the pin into her finger when the knock on her door startled her.

"I had to get out of my room before I drowned in my chemistry homework," Sarah explained as she made her way to Tasha's bed along the few uncluttered spots on the carpet. "What are you up to?"

Tasha picked up her cassette player and began scratching the plastic back. "I'm making everything I own Marcia-proof!"

"You're really serious about this, aren't you?"

Tasha nodded.

"Tell me the truth," said Sarah, sitting on a corner of Tasha's bed. "Is Marcia the only thing that has you mad these days, or does some of this have to do with Billy, too?"

"Billy can do what he wants." Tasha shrugged. "If he doesn't trust me enough to tell me where he goes, I don't trust him either."

Sarah hesitated. "Look, I don't know if I should tell

61

you this," she said. "But Dave found out a little more about what Billy's up to."

"What!" Tasha cried. She whirled around to face her cousin and almost dropped the tape player.

Sarah held up her hand. "Wait a minute," she said. "I don't know much. And what I do know doesn't sound so good."

"That's okay," said Tasha. "I've been assuming the worst since this whole mystery started."

"The other day Billy and Dave were hanging out," said Sarah. "And suddenly Billy checked his watch and said, 'I gotta go; Nora is waiting for me,' and then he left."

"Who's Nora?" Tasha demanded.

Sarah put her hand over her heart. "So help me, I just told you all I know."

"Yes, but is that all Dave knows?" said Tasha. "Call him up," she ordered. "Let's get something more out of him."

Sarah laughed. "I tried, believe me! But he can be just as stubborn as Billy."

Tasha was quiet for a moment. "I can't think of any girls named Nora at the high school. You think she's a college girl?"

"It's probably his boss," said Sarah. "Maybe that's why he doesn't want us to know about his job. It could be that he doesn't like admitting his boss is a woman."

"Billy doesn't care about something like that," said Tasha. "I'm not going to worry about it," she said, hoping she sounded convincing. She picked up the cassette player again and continued scratching the back of it with the hatpin. "Do you want to help me get Marcia?" she asked.

"What do you mean, 'get' her?" Sarah asked.

"Catch her in the act," said Tasha. She pointed to her watch and her tape player. "If she takes something of mine again, the initials on the back will give it away." Sarah gave her a doubtful look, but Tasha ignored her and continued. "You have to admit the girl acts strange. Did you see the way she snapped at Jennifer at 18 Pine today? And how can she afford to wear all that different jewelry? And don't you find it odd that she pulled out a Fiehl pen *exactly* like the one I lost?"

Sarah shook her head. "None of that proves she's a thief," she said. "And I don't think you should try to trap her either."

"Well, I'm not going to let her make a fool of me," Tasha declared.

"Thought I heard you two in here," said Miss Essie. At seventy, Sarah and Tasha's grandmother no longer toured the country with an African-American acting troupe the way she had done years ago, but she still worked in the theater, and made commercials now and then. She had come down with the flu, and the cousins noticed that her usually bright eyes looked dull and cloudy.

"This is for you," said Miss Essie, handing Tasha a note.

"Good for one replacement pen" said the note in

Miss Essie's large looping script.

"Miss Essie, no!" Tasha cried. "It's too expensive."

"Too late," said Miss Essie. "I already ordered it, and it should get here in a few days. Don't worry, child, it didn't cost a thing. I bought the first one with my credit card, which has a theft protection service. I just ordered a free replacement."

"How did you find out mine was lost?" asked Tasha, looking at her cousin suspiciously.

"Never mind that." Miss Essie turned to leave. "Just humor a sick old lady, and don't give me any backtalk about it." She paused at the door. "And when you get the new one, I expect a thank-you note, like the kind you used to write me when you lived in Oakland. Just because you live down the hall doesn't mean you should forget your manners. I want you to tell me all about school, and what boys you are datin', because heaven knows you're not at home enough to tell me in person!" With that, she closed the door.

"Oooh, that woman can fuss!" Sarah whispered. "It must be that flu she's got."

"If it's the flu," Tasha said, chuckling, "she's had it for seventy years!"

Sarah got up from the corner of Tasha's bed and automatically smoothed the covers. "I'd better hit that chemistry homework," she said. "Are you still going after Marcia?" she asked, pointing to Miss Essie's note.

Tasha looked at the note and sighed. "Yeah, but not because I want the pen back," she said. "If she is a

64

thief, Kwame should know it."

"I'm surprised you still care about Kwame after the way he snapped at you at 18 Pine today," said Sarah.

"He was sticking up for his girl," said Tasha. "I can't blame him for that. In a weird way, I was kind of proud of him."

Sarah laughed. "It's funny, but I know exactly what you mean!" At the doorway she turned to face her cousin. "Trapping Marcia now won't prove she stole from you before. I wouldn't try to set her up, if I were you."

Tasha nodded, and her cousin closed the door. She picked up her watch and examined the initials again. "You're not me, Sarah Gordon," she said to the empty room.

18

PINE

Eight

"Whenever I think of my fifth-grade teacher, I get tears in my eyes," said Marcia. She sat on the floor of Kwame's living room, surrounded by cassette tapes. "Mr. Venner was the first man who was ever nice to me."

Kwame held Marcia's hand as he listened to her talk about her strict parents and her mean brother. Mr. Dean had once been a sergeant in the Marine Corps, and he was strict with his children. Now he worked as a security consultant, and his job required him to move every few years. "Mom doesn't work outside the house," Marcia went on, "but she's got a full-time job trying to keep us out of Dad's way when he's around. She's totally afraid of him." Kwame wondered how anyone could turn out as wonderful as Marcia in that household. And I thought *I* had strict parents, he thought.

He glanced at the clock and saw that it was nearly two. The wrestling match was about to start, and he felt guilty for even thinking about it while Marcia was telling him her problems.

"Dang! I didn't want to do this," said Marcia, wiping her eyes with her sleeve.

"Sometimes it's good to talk," Kwame mumbled. He wished he could say something wise and profound, but nothing came to him. "I'm going to get some Kool-Aid," he said after a while. "Do you want some?"

Marcia nodded, and Kwame hurried to the kitchen. When he opened the cupboard, he made a face at the dingy pink and yellow tumblers his family used every day. He pulled out two goblets from the glass cabinet in the living room instead, and filled them to the top with Kool-Aid.

When he returned, Marcia was calm again. "Let's hear this one," she said, picking up a tape. "MC Whack is my favorite."

"I get requests for this tape all the time," said Kwame. He smiled at Marcia's quizzical look. "I sometimes deejay for my friends at parties," he explained.

"Do they pay you?" Marcia asked.

"No, but I go to an awful lot of parties!" Kwame pushed the Play button and watched as Marcia swung her shoulders to the rapid beat of the dance song.

"With all the music you've got," said Marcia, "you could go into business as a deejay."

"You mean this?" said Kwame, waving his hand at the scattered cassette boxes. "This is nothing. You should see the tapes I've got up in my room."

"Can I?" asked Marcia, standing up.

"Uh, actually, the room is a mess," said Kwame, hoping she would sit down again. He didn't exactly want his parents to find him and Marcia in his bedroom. Telling them about Marcia in the first place had been a bad idea, he realized. He could still hear his father whispering to him: "If there's any questions you want me to answer about girls, son, let me know." Worse still had been his mother, who had dabbed at her eyes and said, "My baby's growing up," over and over.

"I don't mind a little mess," said Marcia, walking up the stairs. Kwame picked up his goblet of Kool-Aid and reluctantly followed her.

He pushed open his bedroom door and stepped aside to let Marcia in. At least the bed is made, he thought. With Marcia present, the room seemed different somehow. Objects he had not noticed for a long time suddenly jumped out at him. The shelves that held his prized Civil War souvenirs looked strangely childish. Two caps, a blue and a gray one, faced each other in the center of the top shelf. Behind each one were the artifacts of both sides of the war: bullets, a recruiting poster, replicas of medals, two canteens, and a framed Confederate dollar bill.

"You call this a mess?" said Marcia. "You should see my room!"

Kwame went to his closet and pulled out a bulky suitcase. "The tapes are in here," he said, heading for the door.

"Why go back downstairs?" said Marcia, sitting on Kwame's bed. She patted the quilt. "We can open it here."

Kwame hesitated, not wanting to admit that he was worried his parents would find them alone in his room. "Okay," he said finally. "But let me go get my box—it's got great sound." He ran downstairs, and when he returned, Marcia was busy looking at the cassette covers.

"Most of the stuff in that suitcase is pretty old," Kwame explained. "Less dance stuff, and more jazz. Here, listen to this." He played her a series of songs from his collection, including blues, jazz, and reggae. He was changing tapes again when he heard the car pulling into the driveway. He cursed softly.

"What's wrong?" Marcia asked.

"Nothing," said Kwame, closing the door. He rummaged in his desk drawer and pulled out a pair of earphones. While Marcia listened to the music through the earphones, Kwame pressed his head against the bedroom door and listened for footsteps on the stairs.

"Hey."

Kwame looked at Marcia. She had taken off the earphones and was grinning at him. "Come over here," she said coyly.

Kwame was torn between the desire to kiss her and the need to keep track of where his parents were in the house. The impulse to kiss her won out easily, and he quickly moved toward her.

"Kwame, you in there?" Mrs. Brown's high-pitched voice was unmistakable.

"Yeah, me and Marcia are listening to tunes," he yelled through the closed door. He pulled out the earphone jack, and music filled the room again.

"If you two want a ride to the mall, let me know," said Mrs. Brown through the door. "Your father and I can drop you off on our way to the library."

Kwame opened the door. "Thanks, but we'll probably go later," he said in his brightest, most innocent tone. Mrs. Brown looked past him at Marcia.

"Hello, Mrs. Brown," said Marcia cheerfully. To Kwame's huge relief, she was sitting on the floor, not on the bed.

"That was close," said Kwame when Mrs. Brown had gone downstairs again. Marcia got up to close the door. "Leave it open." said Kwame, "I, uh...was getting a little warm."

Marcia gave him a wicked smile. "I'll bet."

"We can pick up where we left off when they leave," said Kwame. But he could tell from Marcia's expression that the romantic mood had passed.

"Maybe we should get a ride to the mall," she said. "It's cheaper than the bus."

"I'd rather go by bus," said Kwame, going into his closet for his coat. The last thing he wanted was to sit in the backseat of his parents' car, listening to them try to make small talk with Marcia. The thought of his parents trying to sound cool and youthful filled him with dread.

Marcia arranged the tapes in the large suitcase and closed the latch. She picked up the tape deck and looked at it admiringly. "This sure is a nice music box," she said. "Do you think...?"

"Think what?"

"Please don't feel you have to say yes," she said. "But I was wondering if I could borrow it for a while."

Kwame hesitated. Although he let his friends borrow his tapes, he had never loaned his equipment to anyone. The music box he owned was one of the best on the market. It had two cassette ports, a CD player, and a radio with AM, FM, and shortwave bands. It had taken several months of saving his allowance, and a cash birthday gift from his grandparents, to afford it. He looked at his machine, and then at Marcia.

Marcia's eyes were two narrow slits. "Or don't you trust me either?" she said coldly.

"I trust you," said Kwame hastily.

"Sure!" Marcia retorted as she stormed down the stairs. "I suppose Tasha has been telling everybody, 'Don't get too friendly with Marcia—she's a thief!'"

Kwame followed her down the stairs, clutching the tape machine. "Take it!" he pleaded. Marcia ignored him.

"And what about that Jennifer Wilson, with her fancy clothes and jewelry?" Marcia continued. "She acts like she's doing you a favor by talking to you!" She walked to the front door, where she had left her boots, and began to put them on. "Then there's Sarah. Pretending she's a saint all the time."

"Hey, come on!" said Kwame. "You're talking about my friends."

"You don't see it because you're used to it," said Marcia, lacing her boots. "And now their feelings about me are rubbing off on you!" Her voice began to quaver, and she buried her face in her hands.

Kwame knelt down and put his arms around her shoulders.

"I never thought I'd miss Philadelphia this much!" Marcia said into her palms.

"Give my friends another chance," Kwame said soothingly. He helped Marcia into her coat, and when they were ready to go, he picked up the tape machine. "We'll stop by your house first, to drop this off. I insist."

The Deans' house was the smallest on the block in Fairview Heights, which was one of the most expensive neighborhoods in Madison. Still, the house was clean and attractive, Kwame noticed. Inside were dozens of moving cartons that still hadn't been unpacked.

"Wait here," said Marcia as she ran upstairs.

Kwame leaned against a box and waited. Suddenly a door off the hallway opened, and a man with gray eyes like Marcia's emerged. He walked past Kwame holding an empty snack bowl. He wasn't much taller than Kwame, but he walked rigidly, and his hair was trimmed far away from his ears in a military cut. "How're you?" he asked Kwame.

"Fine, sir," Kwame said. "I'm waiting for Marcia to—"

"Good," interrupted Mr. Dean. He headed for the kitchen and reappeared a moment later with a bowl full of pretzels. In another room Kwame could hear a TV blaring.

"Do you know who won the wrestling match this afternoon?" he asked Mr. Dean.

"Nope." The door closed again behind Marcia's father.

Finally Marcia came down. She had changed out of her jeans and wore a pair of charcoal-colored slacks. Kwame inhaled the fresh burst of perfume that surrounded her.

"Do you want to see *Mutant*, that horror movie everybody's talking about?" asked Kwame as they walked to the bus shelter.

"Maybe some other time," said Marcia. "I wanted to check out some necklaces I saw in Gitenstein's," she said. Worth's and Gitenstein's were the two largest stores at the Westcove Mall.

"You like to shop almost as much as Jennifer does," Kwame commented.

"You don't mind, do you?" said Marcia, squeezing his hand.

"Not in the least," said Kwame. He hoped he sounded convincing.

"Don't worry," said Marcia when they were on the bus. "I'll take very good care of your tape machine."

"I forgot all about it," said Kwame truthfully. He suddenly remembered his brief encounter with Mr. Dean. "I met your dad," he told her. "He's... uh... not very chatty."

Marcia laughed. "No, he's not," she said. "But if it makes you feel any better, he doesn't talk to me very much either, except to tell me what to do. Otherwise, I could burn the house down and he wouldn't notice me!"

Kwame listened as Marcia launched into another story about her strict parents.

When they arrived at the mall, Kwame made his way to a bank of pay phones. "I have to make an important phone call," he told Marcia. She waited as he dialed Steve's number. Mrs. Adams answered the phone.

"Steve isn't here right now, Kwame," she said. "He went for a walk."

"I see," said Kwame. "Did he leave in a good mood or in a bad mood?"

"A foul mood, now that you mention it," said Mrs. Adams. "He kept yelling, 'Don was robbed.' What's this all about?"

Kwame quickly explained and hung up. He turned to Marcia with a big smile on his face. "My wrestler won," he told her triumphantly.

But Marcia wasn't smiling. "Is that what this call was about?" she said. "You knew I wanted to get to

Gitenstein's in a hurry."

Kwame looked at her, surprised. "It was just one phone call—it took less than a minute."

"That's not the point!" said Marcia. "I thought *I* was more important than a silly wrestling match."

"You're far more important," Kwame replied, trying to smooth things over. He couldn't believe she was making such a big deal over a little thing like this.

"Because if you'd rather be with your other friends—" Marcia began.

"I'd rather be with you," Kwame assured her. This seemed to make Marcia feel better, and he vowed to be more careful. Meeting Marcia was the best thing that had ever happened to him and he was determined not to lose her.

Nine

On Wednesday afternoon, Tasha met Jennifer in a corner of the Murphy High cafeteria. "It belongs to my uncle," she said, pulling a hand-held electronic device from her backpack. She took it out of the leather slipcase and gave it to Jennifer. Tasha had scratched her uncle's initials on the back of the machine, DG, for Donald Gordon. "If Marcia takes it, it will prove I was right. If she doesn't, I'll take back everything I said about her."

Jennifer looked at it skeptically. "Why would Marcia want to steal a calculator?"

"It's not just a calculator," said Tasha, pointing to

the small alphabet keyboard. "It's also a Spanish translator. Remember when Marcia was complaining about how badly she was doing in Mr. Sanchez's class?"

"She told everybody," said Jennifer, looking at the machine. "She could definitely use one of these."

They watched students stream into the cafeteria. Soon the room was filled with the noise of clattering silverware, chairs scraping the floor, and the voices of students relieved to be out of class. Jennifer nudged Tasha and pointed out Kwame and Marcia as they walked in. Kwame placed his book bag on a table far from where his friends usually sat and joined Marcia in the hot lunch line. Jennifer and Tasha approached the table and put their own books on it.

Tasha handed the translator and calculator to Jennifer. "If Marcia sees me with it, she might get suspicious," she explained. "Sometime during lunch, bring it out and talk about how expensive it is."

"How are we going to leave her alone with it?" Jennifer asked.

"We're not," said Tasha. She caught sight of April and waved her over. "Whoever took my pen stole it in front of a whole group of people," she whispered to Jennifer. "If it was Marcia, she'll find a way to make it disappear!"

"This is a change!" said April, sitting down at the new table. Somewhere she'd managed to find lipstick in the same orange shade as her hair.

"Kwame and Marcia's idea," Jennifer explained.

"Are we playing Musical Tables?" said José as he

78

sat down. Cindy, Steve, Billy, and Robert Thornton soon followed. They put their books on the table and went to stand in the hot lunch line.

When Kwame and Marcia returned with their trays, they looked surprised at the full table. Marcia acted even more surprised at Tasha's apology.

"I lost my temper at 18 Pine the other day," Tasha admitted. "I'm sorry." Kwame overheard this and beamed.

"See?" he whispered to Marcia, "I told you she wasn't out to get you." He mouthed a thank-you to Tasha as he sat down.

Happiness washed over him. Things between him and Marcia were going great, and now everyone was getting along. And Marcia seemed to be making an extra effort to be nice to his friends. Halfway through lunch, Jennifer took out the translator and put it on the table.

"Oh my gosh," cried Billy, clutching his heart. "Jennifer is doing homework! How often do you see that?"

"It's about as rare as a total eclipse!" said Robert Thornton.

"Or a bald eagle," José added.

"Or a bald eagle during an eclipse!" said Cindy. They all laughed.

"Very funny," said Jennifer, without looking up. She looked at Kwame in frustration and held the translator out to him. "It's a Spanish translator and a calculator," she said, handing him the device, "but I don't know how to make the calculator part work."

"Hey, if you need a Spanish translator, just ask me," said José. "And I don't need batteries."

"You don't fit in my backpack, either," Jennifer retorted. Their friends laughed.

Kwame looked at the machine closely and whistled. "It's a Quintex 2001. These machines are expensive."

"I need to use the logarithm key," said Jennifer.

"Just let me get warmed up," Kwame said, weaving his fingers together and cracking his knuckles. His friends groaned.

"That sounded painful," April remarked.

"It's not," said Kwame. "The popping noise comes from little pockets of nitrogen moving between the bones in your fingers."

Billy cleared his throat loudly. "Do you mind? I'm trying to eat over here!"

"Careful, Kwame," Jennifer warned as Kwame picked up the calculator. "It's my mom's and she paid a bundle for it."

As soon as Jennifer said this, Marcia glanced at the machine in Kwame's hands with renewed interest. Jennifer caught the glance and nudged Tasha under the table.

Jennifer read out the math problems, and Kwame punched the keys and called out the answers. The others at the table quickly grew bored of listening to this and began to talk about other things.

"Ooh, there's Janine!" said Jennifer after she and Kwame had finished the homework. When she left the table to talk to her friend, Tasha kept track of the translator from the corner of her eye.

Cindy picked it up and punched the keys absently. She was about to return it to Kwame when she noticed that he and Marcia were lost in a tender, whispered conversation.

"Can I see it after you?" Steve asked Cindy. When he was finished with it, he set it down near the center of the table.

The lunch period was almost over, and Tasha noticed with a sinking feeling that her plan had failed. The expensive translator still rested where Steve had placed it. She went to look for Jennifer and found her talking to a cute senior.

"It didn't work," Tasha told Jennifer as they walked back to the table.

Jennifer shrugged. "Maybe she's not your thief."

"Maybe not," said Tasha with a sigh. "But it was worth a try." The dismissal bell rang and everyone scrambled to claim books, trays, and knapsacks. When the girls reached the table, the translator was gone.

"Do you see it?" Jennifer asked.

"No," said Tasha. She caught up with Kwame and asked him.

"I gave it to Cindy," Kwame told her. Cindy was almost out the door before Tasha caught up with her.

"I didn't pick it up either," said Cindy. "Are you sure Jennifer didn't get it back?"

"Billy and Steve said no, too," said Jennifer when they met up again. For the second time in as many weeks, Tasha found herself looking under tables and chairs. This time, instead of frustration, she felt a mixture of anger and excitement.

At Tasha's locker, Jennifer waited as her friend gathered her books for class. "What did I tell you?" said Tasha triumphantly. "Let's go find Marcia and get that machine back." She closed the locker door with a bang. "And my pen!"

"There you are!"

José stopped at Tasha's locker and reached into his shirt pocket. He pulled out the missing translator. "I didn't see you around when the bell rang, so I picked it up," he told Jennifer as he handed it to her. "This thing is great, even if it doesn't translate Spanish swear words." He frowned at Jennifer. "You should be more careful with your mother's things," he said. "Somebody could have walked off with it."

"Thanks, José," said Jennifer, flashing him a smile. She handed the device back to Tasha.

Tasha opened her locker again and placed the translator in her overcoat pocket. "I'm out of the detective business," she said resignedly. "If Marcia stole my pen, then she gets away with it. I hope it leaks all over her favorite pants!"

"We could always try to trap her again with a bracelet or something," Jennifer pointed out.

Tasha closed her locker. "No," she said. "I've been thinking. If Kwame finds out I've been trying to set Marcia up, he'll never forgive me, even if she is a thief."

"He worships the girl," Jennifer agreed. "Marcia has

made him forget his other friends."

"That's why I don't want to get him mad. The last thing Kwame needs is another reason to avoid us," said Tasha.

As Tasha headed off toward her classroom, she turned to Jennifer. "Do you know any girls named Nora in school?"

"Just Nora Monson," said Jennifer. "She's that big white girl in the orchestra who plays the French horn."

Tasha told Jennifer about the mysterious girl Billy had mentioned to Dave that day. "The only girl I came up with was Nora Monson, too. Do you think she and Billy are going out?"

"Are you serious?" said Jennifer, struggling not to laugh out loud. "Nora could not compete with you. She's not that pretty, and she's not that popular."

"But she's white," said Tasha. "Maybe Billy wants to find out what going out with a white girl is like." Just then, Tasha remembered something else. "And Nora smokes. Billy's allergic to cigarette smoke. That would explain his raspy voice."

"We would have smelled tobacco on his clothes," Jennifer pointed out. But Tasha remained unconvinced, so Jennifer promised she would let her know if she heard anything about Billy and Nora Monson.

18 PINE

Ten

During history class that afternoon, Brian Wu told Tasha and the rest of the class about a huge snowball the senior football players had made on the Murphy High practice field.

"The juniors are going to make a bigger one this afternoon during the activities period," said Brian. "Who wants to volunteer?"

Several hands, including Tasha's, went up.

When the final bell rang, Tasha joined a group of twenty juniors on the practice field. She waved to Sarah and Jennifer, and the three of them waited until a sizable snowball had been rolled.

"Billy would love this kind of thing," Tasha told her cousin as they found a place to push on the ball of snow.

"Keep pushing!" someone called out. "We're only halfway there!" The snow boulder grew quickly, but it was not perfectly round, and when it came to rest on one of its flatter sides, it was almost impossible to move. Sarah and Tasha heaved and grunted along with the rest of the juniors, but they were no match for the weight of the ball. Fortunately, a few more guys arrived, and after a while the ball slowly began to move again.

"What we need is someone like Billy," said Tasha. "He should be here helping us, instead of doing whatever it is he's doing."

"Help us out," Steve called to the Gordon cousins. He pointed to a small gap between two grunting guys. The girls pushed for a while, but finally the boulder would roll no farther.

"That's that," said a boy named Reese. He pointed to the seniors' snowball. "Theirs is still bigger."

"They have most of the football players," José pointed out.

"Yeah, and that heavyweight, Derek Johnson, from the wrestling team," said Robert Thornton. "That guy could kick this snowball into the parking lot!"

"We're not done yet," said Marc Halle. He put one of the shorter junior girls on his shoulders and had her climb on top of the snowball, while others gathered smaller snowballs. "Start packing the snow against it

86

with your hands," Marc ordered.

"Who made you the boss?" said Tasha teasingly.

"I named myself," said Marc, returning the smile.

Linda Plunkett, Marc's girlfriend, stepped in between them and stared coolly at Tasha. Marc and Tasha had kissed several months ago as part of a game, and Linda wasn't about to let them get too close.

The juniors worked until the late buses began to pull into the school parking lot. When they stepped back to look at their work, they saw that the snowballs were almost identical in size. Around them the field was practically bare of snow.

"Okay, you-all," Marc shouted. "We've got five more minutes, so let's pick up the pace!"

Suddenly Tasha noticed Linda Plunkett returning from the school building. She headed for Marc.

"It wasn't in the Lost and Found," Linda told him.

"Damn," said Marc.

"What did you lose?" asked Tasha.

"I didn't lose anything," said Marc. "Someone stole a gold BMW key chain I had on the zipper of my knapsack."

"When?" Tasha asked.

Marc looked surprised. "During health class. Why? Do you know who took it?"

"No, someone stole something from me in English class last week, and I was wondering if the thefts were connected."

"You accused Amanda of that!" cried Linda. "Don't deny it, because I was there." She laughed suddenly.

"And everyone heard how you accused Marcia Dean too."

"Wait a minute. Marcia Dean is in my health class," said Marc.

"Don't accuse her if you don't have proof," warned Tasha.

When they were alone again, Sarah grabbed Tasha's arm and turned her around. "Why did you do that?" she snapped.

"Do what?"

"You made Marcia a suspect again," said Sarah.

"Linda's the one who brought up her name," Tasha pointed out.

"You were the one to say the thefts might be connected. Things got stolen before Marcia came here, Tasha."

"I know that," said Tasha hotly.

"Now you've planted a seed of doubt about Marcia in Marc's mind," said Sarah.

"*Linda* brought her name up, not me," Tasha reminded her cousin again.

"She just beat you to the punch," said Sarah.

Steve, Robert, and José gathered closer to listen to the argument. "More talk about stealing," said Steve.

"Haven't you ever stolen something, Tasha?" José asked.

"This is a private conversation," snapped Tasha.

"I'm curious, too," said Sarah.

Tasha looked at them. "Back in Oakland, my friends and I took candy bars from a drugstore. But I was seven years old at the time."

"Did you get caught?" Steve asked.

"Yes," said Tasha. "My dad saw me do it. He took me to the front of the store and made me put back the candy. Then he made me apologize to the owner. I felt like a piece of you-know-what for a long time after that."

"Lots of kids steal when they're small," said Jennifer, joining the group. "I remember stealing change from my mother's pocketbook whenever the ice cream truck came down the street."

"Your mother's lucky there's no cosmetic truck!" said Robert, grinning. Jennifer scowled at him while the others laughed.

"That's small potatoes," said Steve. "When my parents gave me their old Toyota, I used up all my money to put in a cassette player. When I wanted to buy a holder for my tapes, I didn't have any money. I went to an auto parts store and found exactly the one I wanted, but I didn't have enough for it." He held his fingers an inch apart. "I came this close to walking out a side door with it. The place was jammed with people, and I don't think anyone would have noticed." He saw how intently his friends were staring at him and he shook his head. "I chickened out at the last minute," he said.

"My mother once knew somebody who stole just for the thrill of it," said Robert. "This lady had all the money she could want, but she got her kicks from the fear of getting caught."

"There are some sick puppies out there," José said.

"When I was eight, I used to put little plastic chips in the gum machines. Sometimes it worked, sometimes it didn't."

"What's going on here?" demanded a familiar voice. Mr. Schlesinger stood with his hands on his hips at the edge of the field. The vice-principal had walked out of the school without a coat, and he looked cold as well as stern. "We can't have this on school property," he said, pointing to the two snow boulders. "We could get sued! What if some idiot tried to climb it and broke his neck?"

"We would visit you in the hospital, sir," Marc Halle whispered in Tasha's ear. Tasha bit her lip to keep from laughing.

"Take them apart," Mr. Schlesinger said. "Now! Both of them!"

"But we'll miss our buses," said a voice in the crowd.

"Well, then, you'd better get started," said Mr. Schlesinger, walking back to the school.

"You heard the man," said Marc, pointing to the ball the seniors had made. "Let's tear these down!"

The juniors eagerly attacked the seniors' snowball and trampled it apart. When they saw that destroying their own ball would make them miss their buses, they ignored Mr. Shlesinger's order and left it intact, whooping and shouting as they ran toward the parking lot.

Eleven

Before the homeroom bell rang the next morning, Kwame wandered the halls of Murphy High, looking for someone he knew.

The night before, the Deans had driven Marcia and Kwame to Meylor's, an outlet store a few miles south of Madison. On the ride home, he and Marcia had sat in the backseat. "Open your hand and close your eyes," Marcia had said. She put something cool in his hand. Kwame opened his eyes and looked at a thin gold neck chain. He had never liked jewelry, but his eyes shone as he gazed at it. The gold strand in his palm seemed to blink on and off under the passing streetlights. "It's beautiful," Kwame had whispered. "But it's too much."

"You deserve it," Marcia had said.

Kwame found Tasha and Billy standing near a drinking fountain, and he headed toward them, unbuttoning his shirt to show them Marcia's gift. When he noticed their tense expressions, he stopped where he was and pretended to tie his shoe.

"I forgot, okay?" said Billy, waving his arms helplessly.

"That's no excuse, Billy. I told you about this concert a month ago!" said Tasha loudly.

"You know I'd rather be at that concert with you than at my job, baby," he said soothingly. He tried to hug Tasha, but she pushed his arms away.

"I'm not your 'baby,'" said Tasha. "And if you really want to go to the concert, why don't you call in sick to this job of yours?"

"I can't do that. Someone's depending on me."

"Nora?"

"Who told you about her?" Billy cried.

"Never mind," said Tasha, "I just know."

"Who told you?" Billy repeated.

"I'll give up my sources, if you tell me what you're doing with your afternoons."

"Spending them with Nora!" said Billy fiercely. "At least she doesn't interrogate me!"

"What does she do for you?" Tasha shot back.

Billy didn't answer the question; he simply muttered something at Tasha and strode down the hall.

Kwame watched the big football player walk away, and decided it wasn't a good time to show off his neck chain. He turned to go back the way he came and nearly knocked Jennifer over.

"You're going to ram into someone if you keep walking with your head down," said Jennifer.

"Sorry," said Kwame. "Hey, nice outfit," he said, admiring the navy and green plaid skirt and blue sweater she wore.

"Thanks," said Jennifer. "I just got it."

"You notice anything new on me?" said Kwame, leaning toward her and raising his chin.

Jennifer looked at his throat. "You mean that hickey?" she said.

"Where!" said Kwame, his hand flying to his throat.

"I'm teasing," said Jennifer, laughing. "Mmm-hm, that's a beautiful chain," she said. "Did Marcia get it for you?"

"Who else?" Kwame beamed.

"That girl has some serious cash flow!"

"Yeah," Sarah agreed as she joined them in the hall. "What do Mommy and Daddy do, anyway?" she asked.

"He does some kind of consulting," said Kwame. "They're doing all right if they live in Fairview Heights. But Marcia is just plain generous!"

"You got that right," said Sarah. "She just offered me a pair of earrings. Silverplate. I had to turn them down because silverplate makes my ears itch like crazy."

"Well, shoot!" said Jennifer. "Send her over to me next time!"

Tasha joined them a moment later, and Kwame showed off the gold chain again. Tasha nodded approvingly, but she looked distracted.

Sarah nudged her cousin. "Billy?" she whispered. Tasha nodded. "Fight?" Sarah asked. Tasha nodded again.

"Where did you put Billy's body?" said Jennifer.

"It's not that bad, yet," said Tasha, smiling reluctantly. She turned to Kwame. "I ought to ask Marcia how she keeps you in line—maybe it'll work for me, too."

"Ask her yourself; here she comes now," said Kwame, looking over Sarah's shoulder.

"Hi, everybody," said Marcia with a big smile. She wore a red turtleneck sweater that set off her dark skin and made her eyes sparkle.

Jennifer's glance was attracted by the necklace Marcia wore: a combination of tiny pink cowrie shells spaced with black wooden beads.

"That is beautiful," said Jennifer, lifting the strand with her finger. "Where did you get it?"

"Ms. Tique," said Marcia.

"Do you mind if I ask how much it was?" Jennifer asked.

"To tell you the truth, I don't remember, because I got some other things with it," said Marcia. "Had to be less than thirty dollars."

"Into your homerooms, please; the bell is about to

ring!" shouted a student monitor.

"Are you going to walk me to my homeroom, Musketeer?" Marcia asked Kwame.

With a flustered smile, Kwame waved good-bye to his friends.

Tasha watched them walk off holding hands. "I could definitely use some of that love potion she's got." She sighed.

"Yeah, but she could use some truth serum," Jennifer murmured. The Gordon cousins looked at her, surprised. "I've been to Ms. Tique a million times," she explained, "and I know for a fact they don't sell that necklace she had on!"

"She could have made a mistake," said Sarah. "That doesn't mean she lied."

Jennifer shook her head. "She also said it didn't cost more than thirty dollars, remember? The only place I've seen that style of wood and shell necklace is at the Craft Boutique, out by Meylor's. They don't sell anything for less than seventy dollars. I don't care if her uncle is Eddie Murphy; she'd remember paying that much!"

Twelve

During lunch that day, Kwame showed off his gold chain to the rest of his friends.

"It makes you look dashing, Kwame," said Renee Wright, a girl he knew from math class.

"Thanks, Renee," said Kwame casually. Since he had been dating Marcia, he no longer felt awkward talking to girls, even pretty ones like Renee.

When Marcia left to buy more milk, Steve sat in her empty chair to talk to his friend. "I've got the new *Buzzsaw* graphic novel," he told Kwame.

"It's out already?" Kwame cried.

"It's been out for three days," said Steve. "First

printing, number one—it sold out in less than two hours."

"I haven't been to Comic Collectibles in a long time," said Kwame glumly.

"You haven't been at 18 Pine lately either," Steve pointed out. "Hey, if you want to read my copy of *Buzzsaw*, or play video games or something..." He left the offer unfinished.

"Yeah, we have to get together and do something soon," said Kwame, grabbing a pretzel from the bag Steve had in front of him.

"Careful, man," Steve said. "You don't want to ruin your diet!"

Steve had meant it as a joke, but Kwame sensed sarcasm in his friend's tone of voice. He wondered if Steve was angry about something, but Marcia returned before Kwame could ask him about it.

"What's up with April?" asked Robert Thornton. He pointed with his fork to a table where April sat alone, reading a magazine.

"She's not talking to me." Steve sighed.

"Did you say something about her hair?" Cindy asked him.

"Not a word," said Steve. He told his friends about his fight with April that morning. "She asked me why we haven't been doing anything together lately. The truth is, I don't like to have my girlfriend stared at in public. That's why I haven't been asking her out. But I couldn't tell her that."

"What reason did you give her?" asked Sarah.

"I told her it was her breath," Steve mumbled. The gang groaned in dismay. "It's stupid, I know! But I can't think on my feet, and April wanted a reason."

"No wonder she's over there!" Sarah cried. She walked over to April's table, but when April saw her, she immediately covered her mouth and gestured at Sarah to keep her distance.

"If that's how sensitive she is about bad breath when she doesn't even have it, imagine how she'd overreact if someone told her the truth about her hair," said Steve miserably. "What am I going to do?" he asked his friends.

No one had any ideas.

After lunch Tasha took Kwame aside. "Can I talk to you alone this afternoon?"

"Actually, I already have other plans," said Kwame. "Marcia wants to go back out to Meylor's this afternoon to look at some blouses."

"This is really important," said Tasha. "It's about you and Marcia."

Kwame refused, but Tasha kept insisting. "You're like a pit bull," he told her as he threw up his hands. "Okay, okay. I'll see if I can get out of it."

Marcia wasn't as easy to convince. "I thought we had a date for this afternoon."

"I haven't seen my other friends in a while," Kwame pointed out.

Marcia raised her sleeve and showed Kwame where she had drawn a heart on her wrist. Inside the heart was the name "Kwame." She pulled out a black felt-tipped pen, took Kwame's hand, and drew a heart with the name "Marcia." "Okay," she said, smiling. "Now you can go."

Kwame gave her a quick kiss. "I'll call you tonight," he promised. As he walked away, he felt slightly guilty. He didn't want to admit it to himself, but he was relieved that he would not have to go shopping with Marcia that afternoon.

Tasha and Kwame met at Kwame's locker after school.

"Do you want to talk in the senior activities lounge?" Tasha asked. "It's usually empty after school."

"If you don't mind," said Kwame, "I'd rather walk." He had forgotten to do his sit-ups the night before, and even a tiny amount of exercise would make him feel better.

"Well?" said Kwame as they walked along the practice field. "What did you want to talk about?"

Tasha made a snowball and threw it at a telephone pole; it hit with a smack. "You've been avoiding your friends lately," she said.

"Marcia doesn't feel comfortable around the gang yet," Kwame responded.

"It seems all you two do is go shopping," said Tasha. "Doesn't she have other interests?"

"Shopping is what she likes to do." Kwame looked at the gray sky and said nothing for a while. "You still think she's a thief, don't you?" he said softly.

"I don't know what she is," said Tasha. "But I don't want you to forget your other friends. When Steve and April started going out, did Steve ignore you? Did he stop hanging out with the rest of us?"

"Marcia didn't force me to stop hanging out with you-all," said Kwame angrily. He threw a snowball at the same telephone pole Tasha had hit. It flew wide by six feet. He narrowed his eyes at Tasha. "You're a jock."

Tasha laughed. "I'm also a friend of yours," she said, squeezing his arm. "Who else would have quizzed me on my history final last semester?"

Kwame smiled. "We stayed at 18 Pine until Mr. Harris closed the place, remember?"

"I remember," said Tasha. "But now that Marcia is in the picture, it doesn't look like we'll do that again."

They walked in silence to a neighborhood where a group of boys were playing street hockey. "What does the rest of the gang think of Marcia?" Kwame asked.

"You want the truth?" said Tasha. "Some of them think Marcia is nice and really likes you. But others think it's a one-sided relationship, and she's taking advantage of you."

"What do you mean?" Kwame shot back. "I choose to spend my time with her. How's that taking advantage of me?"

"Have you seen a movie together? Gone to a dance? Gone to the arcade?"

"Not yet," Kwame admitted.

"You always do what she wants, never what you

want," said Tasha. "Looks like a one-sided relationship to me. She's also got you doing things you would never have done on your own: shopping, dieting, and avoiding your friends."

"That's not true," protested Kwame.

"Tell me where I've lied," Tasha challenged.

Kwame whirled around to face her. Ever since he'd met Tasha, he'd been totally enthralled with her. But he was a year younger than she was, and he knew Tasha would never consider him a contender. So why was she giving him a hard time now that he had Marcia? "You want to know the truth? What I think?" said Kwame finally. "I think you want me back, Tasha, not the others. It's not enough that you're dating Billy and flirting with Marc Halle. You want me around, too. You're just upset because I'm not a part of your harem anymore."

"Harem!" Tasha echoed.

"Laugh if you want to," said Kwame. "Tell me where *I've* lied. You love having a lot of guys paying attention to you!"

"Maybe I do like to flirt," said Tasha. "So what?"

"So Marcia is pretty, and to you that's competition."

"You're way off," said Tasha, shaking her head.

Kwame thought carefully about his next words. "Look, Tasha," he said. "I like you a lot. A whole lot. I know I'm not the type of guy you like as a boyfriend, and I would never mess up our friendship by making a play for you, but I have feelings, too. I want someone special, just like you have Billy, and Steve has April.

102

And if that's causing a problem with the gang, I'm sorry, but I'm sticking by Marcia."

"I always knew you really liked me," said Tasha. "But if you think I just wanted you as another admirer, you're wrong. You mean a lot more to me than that. I want you to continue seeing Marcia, and find time for your other friends."

"Is that really what you want?" said Kwame, still suspicious.

"Honest."

"Because that's what I want, too," said Kwame.

Tasha smiled. "I was hoping you'd say that."

Neither could think of anything else to say, and they found themselves embracing tightly. Two weeks ago, Kwame would have gotten flustered in a long hug with Tasha, but now it felt as natural as breathing. They hugged again at the curb in front of the late buses.

"I'm glad we had this talk," said Tasha.

"Me too," said Kwame.

He waved good-bye to Tasha from his seat on the bus. His eye fell on the heart Marcia had inked on his wrist. Tasha is right about one thing, Kwame thought. Marcia has changed me. But it's for the better! And if we're always doing what she likes, so what?

But the more he thought about it, the more Kwame realized that spending all his time with Marcia had unpleasant consequences, too. Going to the mall almost every afternoon meant that he did not spend much time on his homework. His bayonet was now months away because he had spent his allowance, and the advance on the allowance, on Marcia. Nor had he found the time to add the latest dance tunes to his music collection.

When he looked out the window, Kwame saw that the bus was driving past the Westcove Mall. Impulsively, he got off at the next stop and walked back. He wandered through the mall, taking his time to look at the boats that were on display as part of a boat show. He had walked past them several times with Marcia, but she had never let him linger around them.

The video arcade was full of kids from the nearby junior high school. Kwame watched a stocky Asian boy slapping the firing button on the Open Season game Steve liked so much. When the Asian boy lost his last hunter, he stormed off. Kwame dropped his token into the slot and took up his position in front of the glass screen. It feels good to be playing, even though Steve isn't around, he thought as his fingers fluttered on the firing button.

It was Sarah and Tasha's turn to make dinner that evening. Sarah let Tasha set the table while she ran into the kitchen to check on the spaghetti and stir the tomato sauce.

"I talked to Kwame today," Tasha told Sarah when she returned to the dining room. She told her cousin all about the talk.

"Don't you think you were a little hard on Marcia?" said Sarah.

"He has to know we're still his friends," said Tasha.

"I'm looking out for him."

"What did he say?" Sarah asked her cousin.

"What did who say?" said Miss Essie, walking into the room.

"We're just talking about school," said Sarah.

"Good, let's hear it," said Miss Essie, taking her seat at the dining table. She gave Tasha a severe look. "You thought I was kidding about that thank-you note, didn't you?" she said. "I told you I wanted to hear what you were up to. Now fill me in!"

The Gordon cousins took turns telling their grandmother about Kwame and Marcia. Miss Essie raised her eyebrows when Tasha told her about the missing pen and Marc Halle's BMW key chain.

Sarah pointed to her cousin. "Tell her not to be so suspicious and to mind her own business," she said. "She won't listen to me."

"Don't be so suspicious, and mind your own business," Miss Essie told Tasha.

"Okay, but tell Sarah she's naive, just like Kwame, and I don't want him to get hurt!" said Tasha.

Miss Essie fixed her eyes on Sarah and repeated Tasha's words. The cousins were silent.

"So what do you think?" they asked.

"'Bout time somebody asked me!" Miss Essie retorted. "Kwame has never had a girlfriend before, so of course he's going to spend all his time with her. But that early heat don't last, and soon he'll realize that he doesn't have to choose between his friends and Marcia."

"That's what I tried to tell him," said Tasha triumphantly.

"You can tell him all you want, but it won't make a difference," Miss Essie told Tasha. "You can't tell a lovesick person anything. She could be the Boston Strangler and Kwame wouldn't believe it. Give him time, he'll come to his senses. Love makes you pretty thickheaded, especially when you're Kwame's age and you haven't been around the block."

"How many times have you been in love, Miss Essie?" Sarah teased.

"Just once," said Miss Essie piously. "With your grandfather."

"What about before you met him?" Sarah pressed.

Miss Essie tried to hide her smile. "Child, as we used to say, you've stopped visiting and gone on to meddling!"

At one in the morning, the phone rang in the Brown household. When he heard his mother knocking on his door, Kwame stumbled to the phone without bothering to put on his glasses.

"I know it's late," said Marcia, "but I thought you were going to call me tonight."

"That's right, I remember now," said Kwame, yawning.

"How was your talk with Tasha?"

"Good. We got some things straightened out," said Kwame.

"Did she talk about me?"

Kwame didn't want to lie, but he didn't want to stay on the phone for a half hour trying to remember every detail of his talk that afternoon. "We talked about a lot of things," he said finally. "But it was mostly about me."

"I'll bet," said Marcia sarcastically. "If she thinks she's going to take you away from me, I'm going to have to jack her up!"

"I like being fought over," said Kwame. "But don't worry, it wasn't anything like that."

"Do you want to do something after school tomorrow?" Marcia asked.

"Sure," said Kwame. "Uh, as long as we don't go shopping, okay?"

There was a pause over the phone line. "You never complained before," said Marcia, her voice hard.

Kwame closed his eyes and screwed up his courage. "It's all we ever do, and I just want to mix it up a little bit. I was thinking this afternoon. I really don't know that much about you. All we ever talk about is shopping, and your dad."

He was sorry he had said it when he heard Marcia sniffling.

"Well, if I bore you when we talk, and bore you when we go out, I don't know why you hang around!" she cried.

The line went dead, and Kwame stared at the phone in his hand. He squinted at the buttons on the phone to bring them into focus and dialed her number. Abruptly he hung up, afraid that the ringing

107

would wake up Mr. Dean.

"I've got to learn to keep my mouth shut," Kwame mumbled. The phone jangled, and he snatched it before the first ring ended.

"Hello?"

"My name is Marcia Dean," said the quiet voice on the other end. "I like shopping, kung fu movies, dancing, Frisbee, salami and cream cheese sandwiches, popcorn, Siamese cats, raspberry bubble gum, kissing—and Kwame Brown." She paused. "Are you still there?"

"That was really sweet," said Kwame softly.

"You want to come over to my place tomorrow? We won't go shopping," Marcia promised.

"I'd like to see you right now," said Kwame. "Leave the back window open—I'll be the one wearing black-rimmed glasses and pajamas!"

"You're crazy!" She laughed.

After they hung up, Kwame returned to his bedroom feeling satisfied. Maybe he and Marcia would finally do something together besides shopping. He was glad he'd had the talk with Tasha and even more glad that Marcia had called back.

18
PINE

Thirteen

Kwame sat on the edge of the bed in Marcia's room and glanced at the clock. It was 2:15 in the afternoon. I'd be in English class, he told himself. He felt a pang of guilt for having left school during the lunch hour that day, but Marcia had insisted. "We'll have the whole house to ourselves," she had said. "My mom is helping my dad at the office today." Kwame was glad Tasha hadn't seen them leave. To her, it would have been another example of Marcia's making him do something he would never have done on his own.

"Good thing you didn't run over here in your pajamas last night," said Marcia, pointing out her bedroom window, which overlooked the backyard. "Old Sam-

109

son would have had you for a midnight snack."

Kwame looked out and saw a large doghouse in the back corner of the Deans' yard. A hairy mutt sniffed the air a few feet away from it. The brute easily weighed a hundred pounds. "Niiice doggy," Kwame said from the safety of the second floor.

When he turned away from the window, he saw Marcia holding out a pad of paper and a pencil to him. "Remember when Tasha accused me of stealing her pen at 18 Pine?"

"How could I forget?" said Kwame, taking the pencil and paper. "I never finished that personality quiz you asked me to take."

"You can do it now," she said. "Draw a woman, using a combination of ten circles, squares, or triangles."

When he finished, Marcia took the crude drawing and counted each shape. "Very interesting. You used four squares, two circles, and four triangles," she told him.

"Did I pass? Do I have a personality?" Kwame grinned.

"Very interesting," Marcia repeated. She showed him the drawing. "The squares represent your intelligence, the circles represent your creativity, and the triangles," she said with a mischievous grin, "represent your sex drive."

"Wow, my sex drive is as strong as my intelligence!" said Kwame. He smiled at Marcia. "So, how did you do on the quiz?" he asked.

"Three triangles, four circles, and three squares," Marcia replied.

"I'd say we're compatible," said Kwame, reaching for her hand.

"Stay there," said Marcia, standing up suddenly. She disappeared for a moment and returned with a bottle of suntan lotion. Kwame's eyes went from the bottle to Marcia's eager expression.

"Marcia," he said, "it's January!"

"Watch," said Marcia. She flipped the top of the bottle open, tilted her head back, and squeezed a jet of liquid into her mouth. She almost spat it out laughing when she saw Kwame's stunned expression.

"It's wine, silly!" said Marcia. "My brother doesn't want my parents to know about it. Pretty ingenious, huh?" she said, holding the bottle out to Kwame.

"No thanks," he said. It wasn't only drinking the wine that bothered him, but the possibility that her ingenious brother had not rinsed the bottle out before switching liquids.

"Come on, don't be silly," said Marcia insistently.

Kwame hesitated. He'd had alcohol before, but never a lot of it and never during the school day. Ordinarily he had no interest in the stuff, but Marcia was looking at him expectantly. "Sometimes I forget you're only a sophomore," she said.

Kwame took the bottle. The jet of wine tickled the roof of his mouth. "Smooth and fruity—a good year," he said, trying to sound casual.

Marcia laughed and beckoned him to the edge of the

111

bed. "I've got something else for you," she said.

Kwame sat down as Marcia opened her nightstand drawer and pulled out a man's gold bracelet. "To match your chain," she said, handing it to him. She was surprised to see him shaking his head.

"I can't accept it," said Kwame firmly.

"Why?"

"I just...don't feel comfortable taking expensive gifts from you."

"Do you think I stole it?" she asked.

"Of course not!" Kwame protested. "But I feel bad because I can't get you anything like what you give me. It hurts my pride."

"You've already paid me back," said Marcia, "by being my friend." She put the gold bracelet on his arm, next to the friendship band she'd given him the week before.

Kwame tried not to look surprised when Marcia got up suddenly and took off her sweatshirt. Underneath she wore a pink ribbed-cotton tank top. It was tight enough for Kwame to notice she wasn't wearing a bra. She sat next to him, cupped his face in her hands, and kissed him for a long time.

Kwame gripped her shoulders in his hands and returned the kiss. Marcia made his body feel like a summer night before a storm: warm, with flashes of heat lightning.

"Before we go any further," said Kwame in a drowsy voice, "how about some slow music to set the mood?"

"How romantic," said Marcia with a grin.

Kwame pointed to the personality quiz. "Blame it on the triangles," he said.

Marcia tuned the radio beside the bed to a soul-music station. "What's wrong?" she said when she turned back to him.

"Nothing," said Kwame, looking around the room for his tape deck. He scanned her desk and the top of her dressers and every other place large enough to hold it. "I . . . uh . . . was looking for my tape deck."

"You're worried about that now?" said Marcia, pulling him toward her.

"Yeah," said Kwame with a grin. "I want to crank up the bass, and let it kind of wash over us."

"My brother has it," said Marcia.

"Don't move," said Kwame, heading for the hallway. "I'll get it myself. Which one is his room?"

"Let's just listen to the radio," Marcia coaxed. Something about her expression alarmed Kwame.

"What's wrong?" he asked.

"I lent your tape deck to my brother." Marcia looked down. "And he took it to school."

Dread filled Kwame's stomach. From Marcia's tone, he could guess what was coming next.

"He said he took his eyes off it for one minute, and the next thing he knew, it was gone," said Marcia. She pulled a pillow out from under the quilt on her bed and began to cry.

"It's okay," said Kwame numbly as he stroked her back. He reached over to the nightstand and turned off

113

the radio. It'll take a year to get the money to replace my box, he thought.

"I'll make it up to you," said Marcia softly.

"It was an accident." Kwame forced himself to smile. "You don't have to replace it."

"I could make it up to you—in another way," said Marcia, pulling his face toward hers.

"I'm sorry," said Kwame as he guided her hand away from his face. "I'm not in the mood anymore."

Fresh tears welled up in Marcia's eyes. "I can't do anything right, can I?" she said, burying her face in the pillow again. When Kwame tried to console her again, she shook his hand off. "Please . . . just go."

Kwame put on his coat and shouldered his knapsack. "I'm sorry," he said, although he wasn't sure why—it wasn't *her* tape deck that had been stolen. He tiptoed down the stairs and cringed when Marcia slammed her bedroom door shut.

Once he was outside, Kwame filled his lungs with sharp clean air. As he walked the half mile to his house, he thought of Dave, Billy, and Steve. He'd always envied them for having girlfriends. Is this what they go through? he wondered. Having a girlfriend was exciting, but it definitely had its drawbacks, too.

Fourteen

That afternoon Billy Simpson walked out of Murphy High, unaware that he was being watched. Sarah, Dave, and Tasha observed him from Dave's car, which was parked behind a van in the student parking lot.

"There he goes," said Tasha, pointing to Billy's car.

Dave started the blue Dodge and waited for three cars to drive past before pulling onto the road that bordered the school.

"Maybe we should leave him alone," he said half-heartedly. Sarah, sitting at his right, nodded in agreement.

"That wasn't what you were saying at lunch," said Tasha. "You were the one who suggested we follow him."

"I was only kidding," said Dave. "I didn't think you'd try to talk me into it!"

"You two are just as curious about Billy's mystery job as I am," said Tasha, leaning on her elbows between the two front seats. "We're losing him," she said, pointing to the distant car.

Dave pressed the gas. "He drives like a maniac!" he muttered. Houses and businesses flew by. They saw Billy take a right on a road that led past the Madison County Fairgrounds.

"This place always reminds me of summer," said Sarah, pointing to the snow-covered lot.

"Remember that carnival basketball toss they had at last year's fair?" said Dave. "It was definitely rigged. In a real court, I never would have missed those free throws."

"I can't believe you're still mad about that," Sarah said. She gave Tasha a bored look. "He brings it up once a week—at least!"

"If it hadn't been crooked, you'd be walking around with a huge teddy bear today," said Dave.

Sarah groaned. "How many times do I have to tell you, Dave. I love the little stuffed frog just as much!"

The road became hilly, and they saw Billy's car as it reached the top of a rise. But when the road dipped down, the truck between them put Billy out of sight again.

"Faster," said Tasha. "We're losing him again."

"This is as fast as I go," said Dave firmly. "I can't risk a ticket."

A mile past the fairgrounds, they passed a sign for River Run Condominiums.

"There's his car!" cried Sarah. "He's turning in."

Dave braked hard, stopping behind a row of evergreen trees that lined the condominium parking lot. "See where he goes," he ordered the Gordon cousins.

Peeking through the pine branches, Tasha caught glimpses of Billy as he stopped at a door in the corner of the building and knocked. A moment later, a tiny white woman opened the door and ushered him in.

Dave nudged Tasha, who was staring at the door Billy had gone through. "Satisfied? He works for an old lady."

But Tasha was out of the car before he finished his sentence. She slipped between the trees and headed for the brick-colored building. She ducked under the window next to the old woman's door. She heard yelling from inside the house.

"Put your raven locks against my heaving bosom!"

It was unmistakably Billy's voice. Tasha shook her head, as if her brain was rejecting what it had heard.

"I am only a pirate of the sea, but you are a pirate of my heart!"

"What the . . . ?" said Dave, who had caught up with her. He and Sarah positioned themselves under the window as well.

"The fire in your eyes has ignited my loins!"

The three of them raised their heads slowly and peered through the window. They saw Billy standing in the center of the room. The captain of Mur-

117

phy's football team was holding a book in one hand and gesturing wildly with the other. In a seat in front of him sat a smiling old woman. Her head bobbed up and down as she sat listening to Billy's dramatic reading.

"Pinch me," Sarah muttered.

"No wonder he didn't want anyone to know," Dave hissed.

"Bethany slipped from LaFitte's grasp and ran to the prow."

"You kids get away from that window before I call a cop!" shouted a voice behind them. Sarah, Dave, and Tasha turned to see an old man in a window of the building across the yard. "I mean it," he shouted. "Get outta there."

The three of them stood.

From inside, Billy heard the old man's shouts, and he glanced at the window. When he saw his three friends, he cursed, threw the book on the floor, and ran to the door. The old woman watched Billy in complete bewilderment.

"I expected it from Tasha, but not from you, Dave!" Billy shouted as his friends ran to the car.

Tasha stopped running and turned to glower at him. "If you had told me where you were going every afternoon, I would have left you alone," she shouted back.

"I told you it was none of your business," Billy shouted again.

"Billy," said Sarah. "This is as much my fault as it is theirs."

"That's bull!" he said, staring at Tasha coldly. "We all know who the nosy one is."

The old woman appeared at the open doorway and smiled at them. "Why don't you ask your friends inside?" she asked Billy.

"Hey, Nora, do you want me to call the cops?" shouted the man from the upper window.

Nora turned to Billy. "What did he say?"

"He wants to know if he should call the cops," Billy repeated near her ear.

"What the hell for?" Nora shouted to the man. She motioned Tasha, Sarah, and Dave to come inside and disappeared into the house.

The chairs and tables in the old woman's condominium seemed like miniature furniture. When Nora invited them to sit on the sofa, Dave's knees jutted up comically.

"No wonder she's not cold in that little cotton dress," Tasha whispered to her cousin. "It must be ninety degrees in here!"

"Maybe she keeps it that way for the plants," said Sarah. She pointed to a flowerpot containing a long-horned cactus the size of a basketball.

Nora emerged from the kitchenette with a can of peanut brittle, which she handed to Billy. "All my grandchildren love this," she told them as Billy pried it open. "But I have six cans, and they're not coming till Easter."

"Speak up when you talk to her," Billy murmured to his friends as he handed around the open can.

119

"My name is Nora Delvau," she said, sitting down. "Call me Nora."

One by one, Billy's friends introduced themselves.

"It is so kind of Billy to fill in for his cousin," said Nora. "Donny is a church volunteer who used to come and help out when my hip got bad," she explained. "He used to read me stories, and when I got better, he kept on reading them."

Tasha suppressed a laugh of relief. Her suspicions about the French horn player Nora Monson seemed more ridiculous than ever as she listened to this animated and quite beautiful old woman talking about how Billy had helped her. Tasha felt a surge of pride as she looked at Billy, who still looked a little shaken at seeing his friends there.

The five of them talked and ate peanut brittle. Nora Delvau had led a fascinating life. She and her husband had taught reading on an Indian reservation. "We learned to speak the Navajo language," she told them. "My husband and I would use it when we didn't want anyone to know what we were saying."

"I bet it worked!" said Sarah.

"It also worked for the U.S. during World War Two," said Nora.

The four friends looked at her curiously.

"Our forces would have Navajo Indians transmit messages," Nora explained. "And the Japanese who intercepted them had no idea what language it was." She looked at them suddenly. "Is this boring you?"

"Not at all," said Tasha, fascinated. The other

120

nodded in agreement.

But as curious as the gang was about Nora's past, the old woman seemed even more curious about them. "All you hear about teenagers on TV is how worthless they are," she said bluntly. She asked Dave about his basketball scholarships and Sarah about her plans for college. By the time Tasha had finished answering the questions Nora asked her about her fashion designs, her own throat felt hoarse.

An hour later, Dave stood up and looked at Nora apologetically. "I have to get going," he shouted.

"Wait here," said Nora, disappearing into the bedroom.

"Why doesn't she get a hearing aid and a pair of glasses?" asked Tasha when Nora was out of the room.

"She's probably just stubborn," murmured Billy. "Maybe she doesn't want to admit she's getting old."

"Or maybe it's because she wants the company," whispered Sarah. "If she got glasses and a hearing aid, she wouldn't need Donny or you."

"That makes sense," Billy agreed. "Donny comes back tomorrow. I won't have to run over here after school anymore." Billy gave his friends a warning glare, the kind he usually reserved for a defensive player on the other team. "You-all found me out, but nobody better breathe a word about this at school."

"On my honor," said Tasha solemnly. The others quickly agreed.

"Here they are!" they heard Nora say. "Billy, can you come here for a minute?"

121

Billy went to the bedroom and came out with a heavy cardboard box.

"Take them all," Nora told them. "I've read them and I'm sick of them."

The box was full of old paperbacks. Most of them were romance novels, but there were some old *Andy Capp*, *Dennis the Menace*, and *Peanuts* cartoon paperbacks wedged between them. Tasha took the box from Billy's hands and thanked Nora loudly.

"You're not going, too, are you?" Nora asked Billy when his friends were at the door.

"Of course not!" said Billy. "We're getting to the last chapter."

"Oh, good!" they heard the old woman say as Billy closed the door.

Sarah, Dave, and Tasha drove back to Madison under a darkening sky. "That woman was something," said Dave as he switched on his headlights. "Teaching on a reservation, traveling all over...shoot! When I reach her age, I hope I've done half the stuff she's done."

"Me too," said Sarah.

"She's like my great-aunt Evie," Dave went on. "Every time I go to her house, she interrogates me about what I'm doing in school. Old women are curious."

"I guess they want to know what's changed since they went to high school," said Sarah.

When Tasha heard this, she felt a pang of conscience. Miss Essie had been asking her for news

122

about Murphy High. It seemed to mean a lot to her, and Tasha vowed to keep their grandmother up to date as well.

Dave laughed. "It's just as well we promised Billy not to tell anybody about it. Nobody would believe us."

"You got that right," said Sarah. She turned to the backseat. "Hey, what's wrong, Tasha? You haven't said a word in a while."

"I'm fine," said Tasha. She thought about Billy standing in the middle of Nora Delvau's living room, shouting romantic lines as loud as he could. She had discovered a new side of a person she'd thought she knew inside out. It made her wonder if everyone had such hidden facets in their personality. Maybe she didn't know anyone as well as she'd once believed. Not Sarah. Not herself. Not Marcia Dean. Maybe she'd jumped the gun by warning Kwame about spending so much time with Marcia.

Fifteen

The Friday-night showing of *Mutant* was letting out, and Kwame shuddered as he recalled the gory ending. The rest of the movie was somewhat of a blur, since he and Marcia had sat in the back row, kissing in the dark. They had finally looked up when they heard the audience shouting warnings to the beautiful heroine on the screen.

"I wonder if that horse that fell over the cliff got hurt," said Marcia.

"They're trained to do those stunts," Kwame reassured her. "I'm worried about the actor who played the Mutant. I heard he got a bad skin infection from all the makeup he wore."

"It serves him right for scaring that horse!" Marcia replied.

All but the largest department stores in the West-cove Mall had closed for the night. But noise was coming out of the video arcade, which stayed open as long as the theaters. Kwame and Marcia went inside, past the skee-ball lanes and the pinball machines. A white photograph booth in a corner offered customers four pictures in five minutes.

Kwame pulled the screen back and twirled the rotating stool to the right height. "You want?" he asked Marcia.

"I want," Marcia replied.

She sat on his lap as Kwame put the money into the machine. Five minutes later, a strip of photographs spat out of the side of the booth.

"Hey, no fair!" said Kwame, pointing to the strip. In two of the pictures, Marcia had flashed her fingers behind his head, giving him horns.

"You're cute either way," said Marcia, taking the pictures and putting them in her purse.

They found Steve in front of his favorite video game. He greeted them without taking his eyes off the screen. "You take a turn," he told Marcia when he'd racked up several extra rounds.

Kwame expected Marcia to turn down the offer and was surprised when she stepped up to the machine. He wondered if it was a sign that Marcia was starting to feel more comfortable around his other friends.

"Dang!" she said as a duck dropped a bomb on her
unter.

"Go another round," Steve offered.

"Thanks," said Marcia, stepping away from the
ame. "But I wanted to get to Gitenstein's before it
oses."

"Better hurry," said Steve, checking his watch.
You've got less than fifteen minutes."

"I'll catch up in a minute," Kwame called out to
Marcia as she hurried out of the arcade. "Look," he
aid to Steve, "do you think you could give us a ride
ome tonight? Otherwise, I have to call my mom,
nd—" Kwame fidgeted.

"Say no more," said Steve. "No problem. I'll meet
ou guys at Gitenstein's at ten."

"I'll buy you a slice at 18 Pine next time," said
wame gratefully. He sprinted out the door to catch up
ith Marcia.

Gitenstein's was nearly empty when they walked in.
he few remaining shoppers were clustered around the
ash registers. Marcia wandered from aisle to aisle,
olding blouses against herself, examining lipsticks,
nd judging her looks in various hats.

Kwame followed her, lost in thought. He still felt
e pressure of her mouth on his lips from their kissing
ession in the theater. He remembered the kisses they
ad shared in her room the day before. How far, he
ondered, would he and Marcia have gone if he had
ot gotten upset about the stolen tape deck? After Mar-
ia had told him to leave, Kwame hadn't been sure

what would happen between them. But Marcia ha
called that night, and the two had talked on the phon
for the next hour and a half, ignoring the call-waitin
beeps and their parents' disapproving glances.

Marcia brought him out of his daydream with
well-aimed spray of cologne.

"You think that's funny?" said Kwame, picking up
second test bottle.

"Don't!" she said, in a little-girl voice that mad
Kwame's insides melt.

The background music stopped, and a deep-voice
announcement filled the store. "Attention, Gitenstein'
customers. Gitenstein's will be closing in ten minute:
Please bring your purchases to the cash registers at thi
time."

"Let's go," said Marcia. She headed for the exit tha
led to the parking lot.

"We'll go out this way," said Kwame, pulling her t
the entrance that led to the rest of the mall. "Stev
promised to meet us here. He can give us a ride home.

Marcia looked toward the parking lot exit. "I'
rather take the bus."

"Don't be silly," said Kwame, checking his watch
"We'd have to wait twenty minutes for the next one.
Marcia followed him reluctantly.

The steel security gate had already been pulle
halfway down the store opening when Kwame an
Marcia reached it. They ducked under it and ha
walked only a few feet when a burly black ma
stepped in front of them. He wore brown pants an

128

white short-sleeved shirt.

"Excuse us," said Kwame, trying to walk around him. His annoyance turned to surprise when the stranger flashed an identification card at them.

"Walter Ferris," said the man, barely moving his lips as he spoke. "I'm with store security. Would you please step back in the store?"

"What's this about?" said Marcia. "We didn't do anything."

Mr. Ferris gave Marcia a blank look and gestured toward the store.

"What's this about?" Marcia asked again when Mr. Ferris marched them into a room marked Private. The room was bare except for a swivel chair and a bank of television monitors.

"May I see some identification?" said Mr. Ferris.

"Not until we know what's going on!" said Kwame. He surprised himself with his flare of temper. But he felt bullied by this guard.

"I'd like the two of you to turn out your pockets, and you, miss, please place the contents of your purse here," said Mr. Ferris, holding out a wooden tray.

Marcia opened her purse and dumped the contents of it on the tray.

Kwame watched as her wallet, wrinkled tissues, sticks of raspberry bubble gum, hairpins, an aspirin box, and the strip of photos they'd had taken that night tumbled onto the tray. He turned out his own pockets and produced his school ID, as the man had requested.

"Can we go now?" asked Marcia, holding out the

empty pockets of her brother's basketball jacket.

"In a minute, miss," said Mr. Ferris. "I'm going to have to ask you to take off your jackets."

Kwame did as he was told, but Marcia held still.

"What are you going to do, strip-search me?" she demanded. "This is ridiculous! Why do you suspect us? Because we're young and black?"

"Because I saw you steal a pair of earrings," Mr Ferris snapped. "I don't care what color you are, you don't steal on my shift. Now please remove your coat."

"I want to call my parents," Marcia announced.

Mr. Ferris picked up the phone and handed it to her. As Marcia dialed, Mr. Ferris pulled a walkie-talkie from his desk drawer and spoke into it. "This is Ferris, I need Nancy Pellowe in room 2." The walkie-talkie squawked as he turned it off.

"Nobody's home," said Marcia, slamming the phone down.

A female security guard appeared in the doorway. She was a heavyset blond woman with small, mean-looking eyes.

"Do you want to take off your coat, or do you want Ms. Pellowe to help you?" Mr. Ferris asked.

"You don't have any proof," said Marcia, near tears.

"If you like, miss, we can go into the other room," said Ms. Pellowe.

"You're slick, young lady, I'll give you that," said Mr. Ferris, sitting on the edge of the desk. "But this ain't the first time I've seen you in the store. Each time the two of you come in here, we lose stock. That

130

doesn't make me look so good."

"Take off your coat so we can get out of here," Kwame muttered. "I don't want my parents to know about this." He was surprised when Marcia mouthed the words "Shut up" at him.

Mr. Ferris looked at Ms. Pellowe. She suddenly grabbed the material under one of Marcia's coat sleeves and patted it. Ms. Pellowe nodded, and Mr. Ferris went to the phone.

"You two are under arrest for shoplifting," he said. "I'm going to call the police." He shot a look at Marcia. "If you don't want to take off your jacket now, you'll have to do it when the police arrive, is that clear?"

Marcia slowly pulled her arms out of her jacket sleeves. Her gray eyes bored into the security guard's with hatred. The sleeves fell to the sides of the coat, and a bracelet hit the floor, followed by a pair of earrings, a small compact, a comb, lipstick, a sample bottle of shampoo, and two bright orange pens.

Kwame stared at the objects on the floor. Fear prickled the back of his neck. Marcia had actually stolen all that stuff. He stared at her.

"Don't worry," she whispered. "This is our first offense; they'll go easy on us."

"Don't talk to me," Kwame muttered back. He tried to tell the security guard that he had nothing to do with the thefts, but Mr. Ferris seemed convinced that Kwame had acted as a lookout. The guard just snapped handcuffs on both of them and led them out of the back room. As they walked through the store, Kwame glanced at the steel screen across the mall entranceway. Behind it, he saw Steve Adams staring at him in shock.

PINE

Sixteen

Kwame and Marcia were escorted to the parking lot, where a police car was flashing its blue and red lights. The police officer eased them into the backseat of the squad car.

"So, you got caught, huh?" the officer said as he drove. When Kwame and Marcia didn't reply, the policeman shrugged his shoulders. "Don't want to make small talk?"

Marcia muttered a curse, and the officer laughed.

Kwame felt numb. He stared blankly out the window of the police car, counting stoplights, the number of cars that passed, and anything else that would stop him from thinking about his predicament, and about his parents' faces when they came to get him.

The police radio squawked, bringing Kwame out of his trance. The fear he had felt in the security room had been replaced by a burning curiosity. In his mind he saw the stolen items tumbling out of Marcia's sleeves, and then saw Tasha's face and heard her warning voice. Questions filled his head. Why had Marcia lied? How many things had she stolen in the past? Did she really love him?

"Or did she play me for a fool?"

"Did you say something, Kwame?" said Marcia.

Kwame shook his head.

The police station was a modern, glass-walled building in a strip of fast-food restaurants and motels. As he and Marcia were led inside, Kwame saw Steve's rust-speckled Toyota pulling into the parking lot. Steve had followed the police car. It made Kwame feel a little better.

"Wait here," said the policeman, removing the handcuffs and motioning them to a pair of plastic chairs.

Marcia tapped Kwame's foot with her shoe. "Kwame, are you going to talk to me?"

"I've got nothing to say," said Kwame coldly.

"Well, I do," said Marcia. "That was the first time I ever stole anything in my life, I swear to you!"

Kwame stared at her. Would she continue to lie?

"Everybody suspected me, anyway," said Marcia. Her voice cracked with emotion.

"Well, like you said, it's your first offense," he muttered sarcastically.

"*Our* first offense," Marcia reminded him. "They arrested both of us."

"I had nothing to do with it," said Kwame quietly.

"You think they're going to believe that?" said Marcia with a harsh laugh.

"It's the truth," said Kwame. "I'm going to tell them the truth."

"Kwame, please, I don't want an arrest record any more than you do," she said in a soft, high-pitched voice. "You're not going to stick by me, after all we've been through?"

Kwame looked at his shoes. "I'm not the one who shoplifted," he said.

"I can't believe you'd let me take the blame myself." Marcia began to sob loudly.

Kwame felt his resistance weakening, but he forced himself to remember how strongly he had defended Marcia to Tasha and his other friends, and how casually Marcia had betrayed that trust with her lies.

When Mr. and Mrs. Dean arrived at the police station in response to Marcia's call, Mr. Dean gave Kwame a murderous look.

Kwame's fingers trembled as he dialed his own home. He heard his father's voice, and forced himself to stay on the line. "Yeah, Dad? I'm at the police station."

"You're where?" said Mr. Brown incredulously. "Are you all right?"

135

Kwame wished he were not all right. He wished he were calling about a car accident or something else that wasn't his fault. Instead he told his father what had happened that night at the mall.

"We'll be right over," said Mr. Brown. "Don't say another word until we get there."

When they arrived, Kwame's parents were led to a room where a gray-haired desk sergeant sat. Kwame noticed the Gitenstein's security guard, now wearing a jacket and tie, sitting in a chair near the front.

"Kwame, are you all right?" said Mrs. Brown, who looked as if she had been crying.

"I'm fine, Mom," Kwame replied.

"We had some thefts in the store last week," the security guard explained to the desk sergeant. He pointed at Kwame and Marcia. "My security cameras didn't catch them in the act, but I noticed these two were in the store both times it happened."

"What does that prove?" said Mrs. Dean, a short, nervous-looking woman. When Mr. Ferris told Marcia's mother about the sleeveful of goods, she became even more upset. "It's that boy she's always out with," she said, pointing to Kwame. "He made her do it."

"Impossible," cried Mrs. Brown. "My son is not a thief. He's on the honor roll at Murphy High."

"It's true," cried a voice from the back of the room. Kwame turned to see Steve approaching the desk.

"Who are you?" the desk sergeant asked.

"I'm a friend of Kwame's," Steve began. "He's not a thief, he's—"

"Let me talk to the parents first, young man," said the policeman.

"—the most honest guy I know. I could bring a hundred friends—"

The sergeant rapped his hand on the desk. "I said, I want to talk to the parents first."

"—who could vouch for his character, sir."

"If you don't shut up, son, I'll have you thrown out of here!" snapped the sergeant. The police officer who had ushered in the parents ordered Steve to a chair. "Let's hear your version of what happened, son," said the sergeant, pointing at Kwame.

Kwame recounted the whole evening, from the moment they had left the video arcade to the time the security guard flashed his ID card. "I didn't steal a thing," he said as he sat down. The moment he did, Marcia began to sob loudly. Kwame ignored her.

"Were you the lookout?" the sergeant asked.

"I wasn't anything!" Kwame stated angrily. "I didn't know what was going on. I thought she was innocent until that stuff came out of her jacket."

"That's a lie," Mr. Dean thundered. "My daughter wouldn't do this kind of thing on her own."

"If my son says it's the truth, the truth it is," said Mr. Brown, fists clenched.

"Can I say something?" said Marcia through her tears. The sergeant nodded and motioned her forward.

"I met Kwame a few days after I moved here," said Marcia. "And I thought he was really sweet at first. But when we started going out, I noticed he acted strange.

137

When we went to stores, he would put things in my purse—"

"That's a lie!" Kwame shouted. "How can you say that, Marcia?"

"It's better this way," Marcia told him. "We have to tell the truth." She faced the sergeant again. "When I found out what he was doing, I told him I wasn't into stealing. Kwame got really mad at me!" Marcia paused to cry for a moment.

"That's just not true!" said Kwame. "You were the one who had to tell me what 'boosting' meant," he reminded Marcia.

"Be quiet, son, you had your turn," the desk sergeant told him.

"But she's lying!" Kwame protested. "You don't expect me to sit here and take it."

"One time," said Marcia, trying to control her breathing, "he threw a bottle of soda at me because I told him I wouldn't steal anymore. Then he acted sweet again, a few minutes later. I love him, but I was scared to death!"

Kwame couldn't understand why the officer let her continue spinning this fantasy. A wave of dread came over him as he realized that the desk sergeant was listening to Marcia's every word. This was unbelievable. Kwame would be photographed, fingerprinted, and maybe even sentenced for a crime he hadn't committed. The thought of a police record trailing him for the rest of his life, and the shame to himself and his parents, overwhelmed him. "Shut up, Marcia!" he

138

shouted, walking toward her. He wanted to shake her to her senses. "Tell them what really happened!"

Mr. Dean stepped in front of Kwame, his eyes glittering with rage. "Listen, you punk," he said, seizing Kwame's jacket in his fists. "You come any closer to my daughter and I swear I'll—" Mr. Brown pulled them apart, and Kwame grabbed his father's shoulder. His knees felt watery.

"I work twelve hours a day," thundered Mr. Dean. "I mortgage myself up to my neck to live in a decent neighborhood, and then a punk like you comes and tries to drag my daughter down. I won't let it happen, you hear me?"

"Calm down, Mr. Dean," said the desk sergeant. He looked at Marcia. "Are you through?"

"No, sir," said Marcia.

"Stick to the truth!" cried Kwame. But Marcia ignored him.

"I was scared of getting caught, but I was more scared of him," Marcia said. The desk sergeant nodded sympathetically. "Every time he put something in my purse, I would shove it up my sleeve so nobody would see it."

"Is that what happened tonight?" asked the desk sergeant softly. Marcia nodded.

"Now you have your chance to respond," said the officer to Kwame.

"I have nothing to say, except that I'm innocent," said Kwame.

"*Innocent!*" cried Mr. Dean. "You were going to

hit her if I hadn't stopped you!"

Mr. Brown shouted in Kwame's defense, and the Deans shouted back. The desk sergeant ordered the parents to come forward to discuss the matter.

While the parents argued, Marcia glanced at Kwame.

"I hope you enjoy the tape deck," he said coldly. Marcia looked away. Without another word, Kwame took off the gold neck chain and the bracelet she had given him. Then, using his teeth, he undid the knot that fastened his friendship band to his wrist.

"I paid for that," he heard Marcia whisper.

Kwame untied the friendship band and placed it on the chair with the other objects. Then he picked it up again, and looked at it for a long time before putting it in his pocket. Marcia silently watched him. They both looked up when they saw Steve approaching the group of parents.

"Your Honor!" Steve cried out.

"I'm not a judge, I'm a sergeant," said the officer behind the desk.

"Yes, sir," said Steve, nodding impatiently. "Right now, it's Marcia's word against Kwame's, right? But we can prove whether or not Marcia is telling the truth by looking at the video."

"What are you talking about?" said the officer irritably.

"Marcia said that Kwame would slip things into her purse. If that's true, the video from the security cameras would show it."

The officer turned to the security guard.

"I have a lot of footage of those two walking in my store," he admitted. "But I never saw him drop anything into her purse."

"I demand to see that video myself," said Mr. Dean.

"You will all see it at the family court hearing," said the sergeant.

"Wait, Daddy," Marcia interrupted. "The tape won't show Kwame putting things into my purse because . . . because it didn't happen."

"Don't stick up for him, honey," said Mrs. Dean. "He can't hurt you now."

"Kwame couldn't hurt a fly," said Marcia softly. "He's the nicest guy I've ever known, and the smartest. The only stupid thing he did was choose me as a friend."

"That's enough, Marcia," said Mr. Dean, giving his daughter a threatening look. "We'll talk about this at home."

"No, Daddy," Marcia said. "If you paid any attention to me, you would have seen it by now. I've been stealing since I was twelve. I was even caught before, but Mom and I never told you."

"Hush, child," hissed Marcia's mother.

"Is this true?" Mr. Dean asked his wife.

"We won't talk about it here," said Mrs. Dean.

"All right," the sergeant interrupted. "If Marcia Dean is willing to sign a statement confirming what she has said, we can proceed to set a date for a family court hearing." He pointed to Kwame and his parents. "You can go."

But Mr. Brown insisted on waiting until he could see Marcia signing the statement with his own eyes.

Knees trembling with relief, Kwame stole one last look at Marcia and her parents before leaving the room. He still had the faint taste of raspberry bubble gum from Marcia's kisses.

Seventeen

It was Saturday afternoon, and Kwame, Tasha, and Jennifer sat in the back booth of 18 Pine St. waiting for a half-mushroom, half-pepperoni pizza to arrive at the table.

When Billy joined them, Jennifer looked surprised. "No secret job today?" she asked.

Billy winked at Tasha. "I retired yesterday."

"But you still won't tell us where you were, right?" said Jennifer. Billy nodded, and Jennifer sighed loudly as she turned to Tasha. "Some people never change," she said.

Billy spread a copy of the *Madison Courier* on the table. "You're famous," he told Kwame, pointing to an

143

item in the police report. "Juveniles arrested at mall," said the small print.

"Please! Don't remind me," said Kwame, shuddering. Steve had told everyone about the previous night's arrest, but when the gang had asked Kwame for details, he had refused to talk about it—it was too embarrassing.

The pizza arrived, and Kwame put two slices on his paper plate and fanned them absently. His mind was still on the events that had occurred the night before. His hand froze in midair when he saw Steve walking toward them.

Steve had bleached his hair a bright yellow. He waved to the stunned group at the table and got a curious look from Mr. Harris when he ordered his Coke.

"Steve . . . why?" sputtered Kwame.

"Why not?" said Steve. "It's just a temporary hair coloring. Do you think April will like it?"

"Frankly, no," said Jennifer.

"Good," Steve said.

When April joined them, her own red-tinted hair was hidden under a baseball cap. She shrieked when she saw Steve's hair.

"What's wrong, April?" Steve asked.

"I'm sorry, Steve," said April. "I . . . Change it back!"

Steve smiled. "You're just not used to it. It'll grow on you."

"You don't look at all like yourself," April insisted.

"If you can change, I can change," said Steve.

"Besides, it's not a bleach job—this stuff comes out in two washings."

April was quiet for a moment. "Do you have any of that dye left over?" she asked.

"Tons of it!" said Steve, with a gleam in his eye.

"I'll tell you what," said April, handing him her baseball cap. "I'll change back if you change back."

Steve pretended to think it over. "Okay," he said wearily. "If it means that much to you." He took April's cap and put it on.

When Sarah and Dave joined them, Dave sat next to Kwame and leaned over to talk into his ear. "Good news," Dave whispered. "Mrs. Dean is on my mother's church committee, and she knows you and I hang out. She stopped by the house this morning with your tape player."

"No way!" Kwame said softly.

Dave nodded.

"Cool." Kwame was glad to have the tape player back, but he had to admit that it didn't matter quite as much as it once had. Kwame had a feeling that he'd be sorting out what had happened with Marcia for a long time.

"Did you see Steve's hair?" said Billy, pulling off Steve's cap so Sarah and Dave could see.

"Oh!" Sarah cried. "I mean, uh, how...punk!"

"You're too kind, Sarah!" said Steve, laughing.

Tasha noticed the untouched slices of pizza on Kwame's plate. She put her arm around him and whispered, "You okay?"

145

"I've had a lot on my mind since last night," he told her. "I...I guess you were right about Marcia, all along."

"For your sake, I wish I'd been wrong," Tasha told him.

"What am I going to do when I see her in school on Monday?" said Kwame.

"What would you like to do?"

"To be honest, I'd like to avoid her if I could," said Kwame. "At least for now. But someday, I'd like to ask her why she did it." He dropped his voice to a whisper. "At Gitenstein's, when they found Marcia with the stolen stuff, I swear she looked relieved!"

"Maybe deep down she wanted to get caught," said Tasha.

"That's what I thought," said Kwame. "She kept talking about how strict her parents were, especially her father, and I think she was stealing to prove he couldn't control her completely." He shrugged. "That's my guess, but I won't know until I ask her. And I'm not ready to do that."

"I don't blame you a bit," said Tasha. "If you want to talk about it more later, we could take a walk. We'll throw snowballs at telephone poles, like we did before. I'll let you win this time."

Kwame grinned in spite of himself, then sighed. "I must have been crazy to fall for her," he said.

"Not crazy," said Tasha, smiling. "Just in love."

Kwame picked up a slice of pizza and took a huge bite. "Isn't it the same thing?" he asked.

146

Coming in Book 11, The Diary

"Here you go," said Dave, dropping his blue notebook on her desk. He held his hand out for Sarah's.

Sarah's heart was beating wildly. "Did Mrs. Parisi say we were going to trade diaries?" she asked Dave weakly.

"Of course," said Dave. "Last Friday. She even wrote it on the board." Dave looked puzzled as he stared at Sarah. "You okay?"

"Yes," said Sarah. She knew she simply could not trade diaries with him; there was no telling how he would react. "Dave, why don't you trade with Jennifer," she said. "I've already promised mine to someone else." She looked frantically around the room for someone—anyone—else.

"Who?" said Dave.

When Sarah trades her personal diary with a girl in her history class, she shares more secrets than she'd like to—and learns more about the quiet girl in the back of the class than she should.

Should Sarah reveal the girl's secrets—if it's a matter of life and death?